A LUKE KASH WESTERN
2

Spirit
and the Blood

DUKE CHARLES

Spirit and the Blood

Spirit and the Blood

For information about this title or to order other books
and/or electronic media, contact the publisher:
D C Engel
Twin Eagle Promotions
El Paso, TX 79912
www.DukeCharles.com
TwinEaglePromo@sbcglobal.net

ISBNs
Softcover: 978-0-9969673-4-1
eBook: 978-0-9969673-3-4

Printed in the United States of America
Cover and Interior Design: Bethel1808

For my bride and family for always being there.

FORWARD

Truly the time hath come, and now is, for my honest introduction and invitation to this great western novel, Spirit and the Blood, written in a style that places you right smack dab in all the action. Duke Charles has the talent and skill to draw the reader immediately into the story from the get-go. Details of the action, the locale, the heart's truth, combined with the desire for justice and truth blends well with native american spirituality interlaced through this story.

As a retired pastor living in El Paso, Texas, I read this novel by first scanning the last and the first chapters before reading it through in a deeper search for the heart of the writer.

Duke applies the proven method of proper-prior-planning-prevents-poor performance (the principle of six P's) in his writing as well as in the life of Luke, our hero. A truly great writer, Duke applies his story-sharing gift to produce an enticing real-to-life story for those of us who love the western history and western lore.

I not only recommend this book, I hope you have the courage to read the first book in the series, People of the Horse, as well.

I recommend you brace yourself for the entire experience. Spirit and the Blood contains many, many surprises. I'm looking forward to experiencing his upcoming book, Blood and Thunder, coming soon...I hope.

Vaya con Dios,
Ron Thomson
(Pastor) El Paso,Tx.

PROLOGUE

Luke heard Storm and the mules start to move uneasily and, at the same time, Bear jumped to his feet and ducked out the trap door of the wagon. Star moved and Luke told her to stay quiet while he handed her a double barrel 12-gauge shotgun.

"If anyone comes through the back door without an invitation you have my permission to take their head off."

"Don't worry. I'll be fine. You just take care of yourself. Do you hear me?" She asked.

Luke kissed the tips of his fingers on his right hand and placed them on her lips, then he slipped out the trap door on the wagon floor and out of Star's sight.

There were three of them and they had pretty much surrounded the camp. One was in the rocks about twenty yards away across the trail, the second was laying on the ground between the bank and the stream. The third was making his way down the trail toward their wagon.

Luke sent Bear to take care of the one in the rocks while he snuck under the ox cart and around to the stream. He belly crawled into the icy water which was about a foot deep, up the current 'til he was parallel to the dark figure lying on the bank. He pulled his very large fighting knife from its sheath; the only sound was the water running by. The dark stranger never heard a thing as his throat was cut from ear to ear. He bled out in the dirt.

Luke moved stealthily up the bank of the stream to get around behind the third man who was crouched down in some brush about sixty feet away and had no idea what awaited him. Bear was on a large boulder behind the man in the rocks waiting for a signal from his master. The very large dog jumped from his perch and landed square in the middle of the bad man's back, close to two hundred pounds of muscle smashing his chest and large belly against the rock he was hiding behind. The air forced from his lungs, the desperado tried to turn and defend himself, but Bear had straddled him and had him pinned. He managed to get his left hand on the handle of his skinning knife and tried to pull it, thinking he could defend himself…Wrong! Bear lowered his mouth around the man's throat, teeth digging in just enough to break the skin. The man knew he was bleeding and he also knew if he moved it would be the last thing he ever did. He was gasping for breath and hoping the jerky movements weren't enough to set the monster off.

Luke came up behind the man hiding in the bushes and just stood there for several seconds with his hand on the grip of the cut off 20-gauge over and under shotgun in the swivel holster that hung on his right hip. His good friend, Miguel Soto, had crafted it for him and it was his prize.

"What exactly are your plans?" asked Luke.

The man jumped, squeezing the trigger on the Winchester as he fell backward, putting a 30-30 slug through his right foot. Luke kicked the rifle away, then pulled the sawed off gun from his holster as the crook started to regain his composure and sit up.

"So do you make a habit of trying to waylay a US marshal, or is this one of yer new bright ideas?"

"US marshal? Ah crap, ain't you 'sposed to have a sign on yer wagon or somethin'?"

Luke backhanded him across the temple with the barrel of the heavy gun. Thud. The back of his head hit the ground, and he was out like a cheap oil lantern. Luke got a pair of shackles from the ox cart, bound him and left him lying in the dirt. He walked over to where Bear had the third man well in hand, shackled him and brought him back across the trail into camp.

"What the hell is that animal you got there? Is that a bear or what? And where's my little brother?"

Luke just looked him in the eye and said, "You weren't much of a mentor. He's lyin' down by the stream."

"A what?" he asked.

"A mentor. It means someone to look up to… and now he's dead."

"You son of a bitch! You killed my kid brother? I'll kill you, ya bastard."

"Does that mean I'm gonna have to look over my shoulder for you from now on?" Luke asked.

"It sure as hell does ya redskin bastard!" Luke pulled his Colt PeaceMaker from his cross-draw holster on his left hip, pulled the hammer back and shot him between the eyes.

"Wrong answer."

Luke sent Bear out to round up their horses while he and Star worked on a hot cup of joe and watched the big moon move across the New Mexico sky.

L uke and Morning Star had been moving at a good pace since before sunup; the mules just kind of found their own rhythm and settled into it. Luke knew they were making good time. In those days you could find a settlement or a small town just about every forty miles, because that was about how far a horse could comfortably go in a day's travel. Luke saw smoke up ahead. He decided to make camp up along the river and ride into town to see the sheriff. Storm, the big Appaloosa, was happy to be able to stretch his legs. He pranced and danced as they headed toward the town. Bear ran by his side and was just as excited as the great horse.

"Well alright then! You want to run? Let's do it," Luke said to Storm, and gave him his head. They took off and

Luke nearly lost his balance. Every time Storm began to run, Luke was amazed at the pure power that the great animal possessed. Bear was right at their side, smiling. Luke rode into Santa Fe up to the sheriff's office and jumped down from Storm, just dropping the hackamore lead rope on the ground.

Luke walked through the door. "Hey Sheriff! How you doin'? I'm Luke Kash from Taos."

The sheriff rose quickly and shook Luke's hand.

"I been hearin' nothin' but good things 'bout you, young feller. Whatcha doin' in our little town?" he asked.

"Heading for Silver City. They got a few bad men up there making it tough on the citizens."

"Yeah, I heard about that. Are you sure you can handle that trouble all by yerself?"

"Well Sheriff, I'm not exactly by myself." Luke motioned with his index finger and Bear stood on his rear legs, putting his front paws on the sheriff's desk.

"Holy crap! What in blue blazes is that? Is that a bear?"

"Nah, just a pup," Luke laughed.

"A pup? Don't bring him 'round when he's grown!...Pup, my butt cheek!" the sheriff mumbled to himself.

Luke asked the sheriff if he would send a wire to his boss, Brady Simms, in Taos, and let him know that they were making good time. The sheriff assured him he would. Luke said his goodbyes and told the sheriff he and Star were camped just outside of town on the river if he needed him. Luke jumped up on Storm and headed out of town. As usual, the big horse and Bear wanted to run, and run they did…like the wind.

Star had caught a couple of nice catfish and had them cooking on the open fire. She had squaw bread; a mixture of flour, baking powder and water, frying in bacon grease in their lodge on wheels. She had found some asparagus growing wild along the bank of the river, had steamed it and let it cool. They ate with their hands and Bear gorged on the leftovers. Luke spent that evening in the wagon working on some drawings he had started in the last few weeks: a couple of landscapes and, of course, a portrait of Star. He always had one of her in the works. He couldn't get enough of her beauty.

The next morning before sunup, Luke had the team hitched and everything tied down in the two wagons. Star had prepared a quick meal of corn meal mush and jerky, and the best hot coffee ever. He had taught her Momma B's secret to brewing this "blood of life." They moved steady all day stopping every couple of hours to water and feed the mules. Once again, by late afternoon, Luke saw the signs of people along the trail and smoke rising above the trees.

"How 'bout a big ol' chunk of Texas beef for dinner tonight?"

"Can we dress up?" Star asked.

Luke just smiled, "Absolutely girl, anything for you."

They were on their second pot of coffee when the owner of the no-name kitchen on Main Street in Albuquerque came up to the table.

"How was everythin', Marshal?"

Luke looked around, "How did you know?"

"Word travels fast 'round these parts. Got a wire yesterday that you were on yer way."

"Everything was just fine, Mr…uhh?"

"You can just call me Jed, Marshal."

"That was my pa's name," Luke said, and he tossed him a $20 gold piece.

"I can't change that, Marshal. Sorry!"

"Don't be sorry, and I don't need any change. You earned it."

"That's enough money to eat on fer a week. Next time yer this way, it's on me. Ya hear?"

"I'll hold ya to that," Luke replied, and while they were sippin' their coffee, Jed showed up with two large bowls of hot peach cobbler, and life was good.

CHAPTER 2

It was twenty-four miles to the little farming town of Santa Belen, and just about eleven o'clock when it came into view. Luke and Star got a whiff of something wonderful on the breeze.

"What the heck is that?" Luke asked, "I gotta find out."

He pulled the mules up along the Rio Grande and unhitched them so they could drink and graze. There were about eight mud huts along the river, and each one had a fire out front with an old woman working around a big cast iron pot. The aroma was marvelous. Luke had never smelled anything like it. He walked up to the nearest fire and asked the old lady what she was cooking. She just smiled, revealing a mouth without many teeth.

She replied, "No comprendo, señor."

"Oh yeah, Mexican… I should have known," he thought to himself.

He made the universal sign for "eat" putting his fingers to his mouth, and the old lady smiled her toothless smile.

"Si señor, no hay problema."

Luke looked at Star and signaled for her to bring the wooden bowls. They ate Chile Verde with pork, fresh flour tortillas and refried beans. He was in heaven and Star wasn't far behind. Luke gave the old lady a $10 gold piece and she tried to refuse, but he insisted. Tears came to her eyes and she came to Luke and kissed him on the cheek. As they were walking back to the wagon, the old lady came to them with a large parcel filled with six very large tortillas rolled up with something inside.

The old lady said, "Burritos."

Puzzled, Luke pointed toward the mules and asked, "Burros?"

She laughed, "Si, burritos. Si señor!"

While she was saying good-bye to Star, Luke took a $50 gold piece from his poke and dropped it in the pocket of the old lady's apron.

They crossed the Rio Grande at a shallow spot downstream and headed on their way southwest into Navajo Indian country. The trail got smaller and rougher, but the mules, Thunder and Lightning, didn't slow as they began to climb. They never showed any sign of tiring, but Luke stopped and pulled them up. He got more harness from the ox cart and hitched Star's big grey and Storm ahead of them just to keep the going easy.

The last couple of hours, Luke was uneasy with the feeling they were being watched. Bear confirmed his suspicions by running up along the wagon and giving a low bark.

"Yeah, I know boy. Just stay alert."

Luke told Morning Star to put his long rifle and shotgun between their legs so they'd be ready. They were always loaded. That evening they camped by a perfectly clear stream a few miles from the small village of Magdalena in the Gallinas Mountains. Luke and Bear walked around the camp and hung out some cans on string with rocks in them about six inches off the ground. He covered the twine with fresh grass. He wasn't sure if these indians were privy to all the skills his father had taught him.

"I guess we'll find out," he thought.

About midnight, a couple of the cans made a very soft rattle—so soft that most people wouldn't hear—but Bear and Luke heard. They dropped down the trapdoor to the ground and Luke was almost startled by a voice from some distance away.

"Little brother, don't be afraid. We come in peace."

Luke asked, "Are you the ones that have been following us all day?"

"Yes, little brother. We mean you no harm."

"Come into my camp. I have food to share," he offered.

Luke stood still as four indians slowly entered the camp from different directions. They weren't wearing war paint, but they were definitely dressed for traveling: full buckskins, calf-high moccasins, full quivers and bows, and wool blankets draped over their horses' necks. The leader had an old Winchester 30-30 in need of much repair. Star prepared the leftover burritos and hot coffee with fresh spring water, and the indians ate while Luke cleaned and made a couple of repairs on the leader's rifle. He reloaded it and handed it back, and the chief nodded his appreciation. Luke and the chief talked late into the night.

"Walks With Bears, you could be in great danger," the chief told him. "I have heard of much trouble up the great mountain. My braves will stay with you for two moons."

Luke asked the chief how he knew his Ute name, and the chief replied, "Every tribe along the great river knows of Walks With Bears and the great stories: how he killed a giant grizzly with just a tree branch; how he catches and tames horses with just his hands. We have heard about the fire stick at his side and, of course, the great dog.

Bear growled and laid his head on Luke's foot.

Luke smiled, "Some things are not as the stories are told my friend."

Star slept, even as the other three indians walked around the camp and looked in the wagons. They looked at the pots and supplies and touched things curiously. They had never seen anything like them before.

Luke rested about three hours, and when Star woke he was backing the team of mules up to the wagon.

"Good morning, my love. How are you?" she asked.

"I'm fine, but there might be some trouble up ahead. You need to be very alert from now on."

Morning Star made a large pot of cornmeal mush with dried beef in it, squaw bread with honey and coffee, and as the sun came up they all ate and prepared for the day. Star spoke to the braves in their native tongue and they laughed.

The braves felt very close to her. Bear got his share and he grunted as he ate, tail wagging. The chief talked with Luke in private for a short time, then nodding to Star, mounted his horse and disappeared back into the tall pines the way they had come. Luke and Star broke camp and climbed aboard the wagon. He snapped the reins above the team's backs and they were off. He explained to Star that the three braves would be traveling with them for two days, and that they probably wouldn't see them, except at night for meals, unless there is a problem.

CHAPTER 3

The four pulling the wagon made steady time up the mountain, better than Luke could have imagined. Late that afternoon, Luke found a clearing under the pines by the fast-running stream. He maneuvered the wagons into position so he could hitch the team and pull onto the trail in the morning. Luke could see large trout swimming against the current, and his mouth began to water. He hadn't eaten since sunup. Morning Star asked when she should have the meal ready.

Luke said, "When it's ready, our friends will be here."

She had prepared a half a dozen very large grilled fish, squaw bread, nuts and fresh berries. Just as she removed the fish from the fire, the three braves rode into camp as if the dinner bell had rung. The five ate in silence. It was customary for the braves not to speak to squaws in the presence of the leader. Luke was obviously in charge and they were in awe of him.

After the meal, Star took the wooden bowls to the stream and scrubbed them with sand, then rinsed them with clean water. Luke spoke with the three braves and they told him of what they had seen and heard that day, and that there might just be some trouble later that night. Luke had heard the drums in the distance during the day but wasn't exactly sure what the message was. The indians told him that riders were coming down the mountain, and that they should be prepared. Luke asked the braves if they were familiar with the workings of the Winchester rifle. They assured him they were, although they didn't have one of their own. He left the campfire for a few minutes and returned with three 30-30 rifles and a leather pouch full of ammunition. The indians' eyes shot wide open as Luke handed each one a Winchester, and the one that seemed to be in charge, the bag of ammo. Luke told them how much he appreciated their company and that the rifles were his gift to them for all their help. They were hooked. They would be Luke's friends for life.

"You can never have enough indian friends," Luke thought to himself, and he smiled.

At around 2AM, Luke heard a light scraping on the wagon. He was already awake. He and Bear had heard the noise in the distance as well. He gently shook Star awake and put his finger to his mouth, signalling her to be very quiet and she nodded that she understood. He handed her a 12-gauge shotgun and a leather bag of shells, and told her to stay in the wagon and be alert. Luke and Bear slipped through the trap door in the bottom of the wagon and crawled to the back of the ox cart before they peeked out. The head brave was standing at the back of the cart and Luke touched him on the shoulder. The indian nodded. Pointing up the trail, he made a sign with his hands that there were twelve riders about two hundred yards away. Luke knew the other two were out in the forest in position to defend the camp. Luke gestured for the indian to go and take a position. Then he checked his Sharps 52-caliber long rifle and laid it on top of the cover of the ox cart along with his Winchester. He had his 20-gauge sawed off in his holster, his fighting knife in its sheath and his Colt PeaceMaker in his cross-draw holster on his left hip.

"Alright!" he said to himself. "If you want to dance around my fire, here it is!" He sent Bear off to his left to get behind the on-coming riders. There were exactly twelve Mexican bandidos coming slowly and very quietly down the mountain just off the trail; but they were expected.

"Ju should be ready, amigos. De camp is just ahead. We are not here to take prisoners so ándale, and we can get back to our casas for frijoles and tort..." The bandido leader was still whispering as a 52-caliber bullet from Luke's long rifle ripped through the chest of the rider to his right. He flew backwards off his horse like he had been hit by a locomotive, dead before he hit the ground—a hole the size of a coffee cup in his chest and the size of a dinner plate in his back. The riderless horse panicked and began to buck. This made the other horses nervous and they started to spin and turn out of control. The other three indians began to fire from their hiding places and the bandidos started to turn their mounts.

There was complete chaos among the bad guys. The leader spun his horse around and headed up the mountain as Luke's second shot ripped into his right shoulder, tearing through flesh and bone. He screamed out loud almost falling off the right side of his horse. He grabbed the saddle horn with his left hand and steadied himself as he jabbed his spurs hard into his horse's flanks. The panicky horse headed up the mountain with all its power, but the fear it was feeling was draining its strength. Just as the bandido thought he had made his escape, WHAM! Bear sailed through the darkness, knocking him to the ground and landing on the gaping wound in his right shoulder. The pain was so great that he passed out and Bear headed back down the trail to rejoin the fray. Luke grabbed his Winchester and began firing, hitting two riders. They both fell to the ground and were trampled by the spooked horses' hooves.

It didn't take Luke long to realize that the indians weren't as proficient with the rifles as they claimed to be. Luke could hear and see chunks of bark being knocked off the pine trees, and very little damage to the bandidos; but the noise from their guns kept the bandidos off guard. The three indians did manage to hit two Mexicans and scare the living hell out of the rest. Two of the indians realized they were not hitting their targets, and dropped their guns. They took up their bows and bandidos started falling with arrows in their chests. Bear jumped from the ground to the back of one of the horses that still had a rider, his big mouth closing around the neck of the Mexican bandit as he dragged him to the ground, breaking his neck in the fall.

As close as Luke could tell, there were only two bandidos left and they were doing their best to get back up the mountain; their horses stepping on anything in their path: legs, heads and bodies, without a second thought. If they weren't dead from the fight, they definitely were now. He took up his long rifle and drew down on the animal trying to climb the mountain. He squeezed the trigger gently and the big gun exploded. The horse reared up on its back legs, fell over and began to roll down the trail, the rider jumping off just before the animal collapsed.

Luke hollered out, "Star! Are you ok?"

"Yes! Yes, I'm fine," she replied. "Can I come out now?"

"Yes, but be very aware of what's going on around you."

She opened the back door of the wagon and was looking directly into the eyes of an undetected bandido. In one very smooth motion, she lifted the barrel of the 12-gauge and pulled the trigger. The Mexican's head vaporized and his body collapsed between the two wagons. Luke ran from his position up the trail back to the wagon and saw Star standing in the doorway, smoking shotgun in her hand. He looked at her and she just shrugged.

By the time the three indians returned with the bandidos' horses and rigs, Star had a pot of coffee ready. The fire was going and a pot of corn meal mush was cooking with squaw bread frying next to it. They ate rapidly and got back to cleaning the area and preparing for the day's travel. Luke gathered some of the pistols and rifles and let the indians keep a number of the weapons. One of the indians strung the bandidos' horses together in a remuda to take back to the village. The other two stayed with Star and Luke as they traveled south.

They finally reached the mountain crest and started down the other side to the Black range. They camped that evening beside a small stream at the base of the Gila forest. They ate fresh fish, some green vegetables that Star had found in the woods, and some berries and nuts. Luke began to realize that Star could find a feast in the middle of a barren desert. Bear decided he was in the mood for rabbit and did a little hunting on his own. Luke inspected the mules and the two horses, and realized that they were in better shape than he and Star. The animals were doing exactly what they were meant to do and enjoying every minute of it. The next morning the indians ate a cold meal of jerky, nuts and berries, said their good-byes to Luke and Star and headed back toward their camp. They had reached the boundary of the Navajo lands. They were about two days' hard ride from Silver City, as close as Luke could tell from the map that Marshal Brady Simms had given him.

CHAPTER 4

Two days later, at around two in the afternoon, they came out of the Mimbres Mountains and into the north end of Silver City. Luke found a grassy field next to the Mimbres River and placed the wagons in a secluded area under some large oak trees. He turned Storm and the mules loose to graze and Bear laid down in the long green grass for a few winks. Star fixed a meal and they ate and talked until Luke said, "Well I guess it's time to make an appearance."

Star asked, "Should I come with you?"

"No! Just stay here and get some rest. I'm sure I'll need your help soon enough." He kissed her on the forehead and whistled for Storm. He came running with the big dog close on his heels.

As he rode off, he hollered back at Star, "Keep that shotgun with you!" and she waved.

Luke reined Storm up to the hitching post in front of the sheriff's office and hopped down. He took the US Marshal's badge out from under his buckskin shirt and let it hang down as he entered the small office. There was a heavy-set man that looked to be past his prime. His face was bruised, his left arm was in a sling and he had a dirty bandage around his head with dried blood on the left side. He was leaning back in his chair and Luke wasn't sure if he was dead or alive. The old man snored and woke himself up. He looked at Luke and tried to focus and clear his throat. Luke just stood there.

"AAH whata! I mean…a what's up, ah Marshal?" he asked as he stood up from his chair.

"Marshal Kash from Taos. How ya doin', Sheriff? Looks like you've had a spell of bad luck."

"Yeah well, it has been a little rough around here fer a while and I'm getting a little tired of gettin' my ass kicked. I'm Macky Shaw," he said.

They shook hands and the sheriff sat back down in his chair a little harder then he meant to. Luke heard him grunt.

"Anything I can do for you sheriff?"

"Nah! I'll be OK. Just watch yer ass. I wish I could get yer back, but I'm a little banged up right at the moment."

"Just sit back and rest and I'll bring a bottle of sippin' whisky by before I head back to camp."

"Ah pardner, that would be a Godsend. I'll look forward to havin a slurp with ya." the sheriff said.

"Where do ya think I need to start?" Luke asked.

"Well, most of the bad guys seem to gather at the saloon just across the street. There's always a couple of 'em there at any time."

"Who can I trust over there?"

"Eddie's the bar tender and owner. He's a good man, but he's scared as hell and his son, Russ, is kinda shatterpated; but he means well."

"Thanks Sheriff. I'll be back."

"You be awful careful young fella."

"I will, Sheriff. See ya soon."

With his Winchester in his left hand, Luke walked across the street, up the step to the wooden walk and through the swinging doors. He did a quick look around and moved to the right corner of the bar so no one would be at his back. He set his rifle down hard on the bar so everyone in the place heard it.

"What'll it be stranger? Uh, I mean Marshal."

"Are you Eddie?" Luke asked.

"Ahhh, yes sir, I am."

"Well Eddie, you can call me Luke and I'll have a beer, if it's cold."

"Yes sir. It's really cold, sir," and he headed to the back room.

"Call me Luke."

"Yes sir, I will." and he disappeared. Luke looked at two cowboys at the other end of the bar. They were drinking whisky and beer, and it looked like they had been at it for the better part of the day; maybe not drunk but definitely slower senses than normal. Eddie showed up with a very large mug of ice-cold beer. Luke said thanks and asked if the two at the end of the bar were part of the troublemakers. Eddie shook his head in the affirmative. Luke took a sip of the cold brew and it went down so good.

Luke stared at the two without saying a word but somehow they felt the fire of his stare.

"Somethun' we can do fer you, mister?" as the one closest to him turned to his right to face Luke.

"That's Marshal to you," Luke replied.

"Boy are you in the wrong place, unless you have about a hundred folks in yer pocket."

"Nope…just me, and I understand yer part of the problem around these parts."

"What problem would that be, Marshal?"

"How about the claim jumpin', robin', thievin' and killin' for openers?"

"Ok yeah," one of the cowboys chuckled, "…and how 'bout pistol whippin' an officer of the law?"

The two just smiled and started to step aside so they both had a clear view of the Marshal.

"What's yer plan, Marshal?" asked the one closest to the bar.

"Well, I thought we'd walk on over to the jail and put you fellas to bed."

They laughed. "Truly?" the other one inquired.

"Truly," Luke replied. "I only ask once, and that was it…. Eddie," Luke said without turning "how much is the bar tab for these hombres?"

"Eddie answered in a low shaky voice, "Altogether 'bout 300 dollars. Nobody's paid a penny for months."

"Well boys, you want to empty yer pockets or you want me to do it for ya?"

The two saddle tramps looked at each other and one said, "Think we'll just drink on you fer a spell," as they both reached for their shooters.

They never cleared leather. The 20-gauge roared and the eight pieces of lead from each barrel hit them in the chest, tearing through flesh and bone, and kept right on going through the heart and beyond. They fell backwards on the old rotted wood floor, blood seeping down between the slats. Luke reloaded, took a swallow of cold beer then casually walked over, unbuckled their holsters and emptied their pockets, putting the contents on the bar. It looked as if they had just been paid. They each had a couple of fifty-dollar gold pieces, a couple of twenty-dollar pieces and some silver dollars. Luke counted the gold and made note, "$280." He jotted on the piece of paper "On account" and slid the gold coins toward Eddie.

"This should help ya get back on your feet." Eddie tried to smile but all that came out was a gurgle.

He finally regained his composure and exclaimed, "Marshal, I'm afraid you just started one hell of a shit storm."

"Well," Luke replied. "I guess that's my job."

Bear stuck his head through the swinging doors and barked loud enough that all the other men in the saloon turned to see what the hell that was. Some of them actually stood on their chairs thinking the animal was coming after them.

Luke said, "It's all right boy, get back to camp and stay with Star."

Bear gave a grunt and backed out the doors then headed up the street towards the river. Luke bellied up to the bar and had a swallow of cold beer. "How many more?" he asked Eddie.

Eddie thought for a couple of seconds, then answered, "…'bout twelve or thirteen close as I can tell. There'll be a half a dozen in here before the day's over."

"OK. Don't tell them I'm in town. I'm sure they'll figure it out on their own before long. Do ya have an undertaker in town?"

Eddie nodded his head, "I'll send my boy, Russell, to fetch him."

Luke tossed a twenty-dollar gold piece on the bar saying, "Give this to the gravedigger and tell him not to leave town. This is gonna be a busy week for him…. Have ya got any good whisky?"

Eddie nodded his head again, "Sure do….some really smooth stuff from back east. They call it brandy."

"Let me have a couple of bottles," and Eddie disappeared once again to the back room. Luke slung the dead men's holsters over his left shoulder as Eddie returned with two very fancy bottles of French brandy.

"How much?" Luke asked.

"Normal eight dollars, but for you, Marshal, you're on the top of my list. If you live, all yer drinks are on me… forever."

Luke smiled and thanked him, picked up the two bottles and headed for the sheriff's office. As he stepped out on the boardwalk, he saw the sheriff peeking through the window. When he saw Luke come out the saloon door, Macky turned and walked out the office door onto the sidewalk to greet him.

"Sorry I missed that," the sheriff exclaimed.

"You didn't miss much, just a couple of bad men going to meet whoever they pray to,… maybe purgatory. I don't know and don't really care…. How about a drink, sheriff?"

"Thought you'd never ask. What the hell ya got there, young fella?"

"It says it's brandy from France, and it's not cheap."

"Well, let's get one of 'um open and find out if it's worth the money," the sheriff replied.

Luke popped the cork as Macky got out a couple of semi-clean tin cups and Luke poured a generous serving in each. They both sniffed the cups, then each took a swallow. Macky was the first to speak.

"Damn! That's somethin' special right there!"

Luke had a slight grin on his face, "Yeah! It sure is. I was gonna leave both these bottles with you, Sheriff, but you'll have to get by with one 'til I get back."

"Not a problem, young Luke. You just be careful and check with me afore ya go marchin' around town. I got a few folks that keep me informed as to what's happenin'."

"OK, Macky. I'll be back in a couple of hours." You just stay out of sight and stay safe." Luke jumped off the sidewalk and landed with one foot on the hitchin' post and slung the other over Storm's back. He settled down and put his knees up against the big horse's shoulder, and they were off. The hackamore rope floated back towards Luke and he caught it in his left hand. Storm was ready to run.

"Let's go find Star, big fella."

Luke was about a quarter mile from camp when he heard shotgun fire. He kicked Storm in the flanks and he moved to that special speed that very few horses had. Luke saw three mounted men in the river shooting at the wagon, but no fire being returned. His heart sank. He pulled up the Winchester slung across his back and readied himself to fire. Just then he saw Star stand up from behind a scrub brush growing along the river. He saw the big 12-gauge go off, knocking her backward about a half a step and he giggled to himself. The lead rider caught enough of the blast that it knocked him off his horse and he landed head-first in the shallow river, breaking his neck. Luke saw Bear come from out of nowhere. He took one step in the water, then up-and-knocked the second rider over backwards and into the river. That left only one. Storm was still running when Luke dropped the rein of the hackamore and leveled his rifle to a spot on the last rider's chest. He squeezed the trigger. The horseman just sat there like nothing had happened, but Luke knew better. Storm slid to a stop and Luke jumped down, watching the last rider in the river. All of a sudden, he slid to one side and fell into the water, dead from now on. Bear came out of the river, leading the three attackers' horses. One was a very good strawberry roan and the other two were worn-out nags. Luke kept the tack and the roan and turned the other two loose to return to wherever the bad guys called home.

"Not a bad afternoon's work…five down and seven, maybe eight to go," Luke thought as he walked towards Star. They embraced.

"Are you OK? What happened?"

"Bear heard them coming so we crawled under the wagon, through the tall grass and down to the stream. He heard you coming and that's when I shot the first one. He's a great friend," she rubbed his head and he licked her hand.

Luke hugged her and told her,"We're going into town."

He gave her a pouch of 12-gauge shells and checked her shotgun. They left the new roan to graze along the river with the mules. Luke knew they would stay and figured the new horse would hang around as well. Star mounted the big gray and Luke jumped up on Storm, and they headed for town with Bear running by their side.

CHAPTER
5

A few minutes later, they were in front of the sheriff's office. Luke introduced Star to Macky and instructed her to stay in the office until he called her out.

"Anything new I should know about, Sheriff?" Luke asked.

"There's at least three in the saloon and one in the bath house down the street."

Luke slipped out the rickety wooden door of the sheriff's office and moved down the street, checking every window as he passed. Everything seemed quiet. There were two horses tied up in front of the bath house. Luke noticed they had been ridden hard and needed some serious care.

He crossed the street and walked between the horses, untying and dropping their reins to the ground. Luke set his Winchester against the old, dried barnwood siding of the bath house so he could grab it on his way out if he needed to make a hasty retreat. He walked in the door, almost without a sound. The barber looked up and Luke put his forefinger to his mouth to signal his silence. He patted his Marshal's badge and the barber shook his head that he understood. The man the barber was working on had a hot towel over his eyes and his heavy beard was lathered. Luke walked up behind the barber's chair, pulled his Colt pistol from his cross draw holster. He struck the hombre across the face through the hot towel with the butt of his pistol; probably harder than necessary. Blood began to seep through the clean white rag.

Luke gestured to the barber, "Where's the other one?" and the barber pointed to a door down the hall. Luke motioned towards a chair and the barber moved quietly and sat. Luke's moccasins were silent as he moved down the hall to the first door. He stopped just outside the room with a big copper tub and took a deep breath, not sure what awaited him on the other side. There was no knob on the door so Luke just pushed it open. He stood there staring into the barrel of a Colt 44.

"Can I he'p ya, mister?" the man in the tub inquired.

Luke breathed easy because he noticed the hammer on the pistol had not been cocked. Bad mistake!

"It's Marshal Kash, and you can drop that shooter or die in your bath."

The bather began to smile and Luke saw his thumb twitch. That's all it took for Luke to make his move. He grabbed the grip of the sawed off over and under, pushed down and squeezed the trigger in one smooth motion. The man's left shoulder and chest exploded and his head began to swell from the lead slugs smashing through skin and bone. He didn't get close to pulling the hammer back or getting a shot off. Luke turned, replacing the 20-gauge shell and walked back through the barber shop.

"Is there a back door?" The barber shook his head in the negative.

Luke never hesitated. He walked out the door and retrieved his Winchester as he passed the window, hugging the front of the wooden buildings as he moved back up the street to the saloon. Just as Luke reached the corner of the saloon, Star's 12-gauge exploded from across the street The swinging doors in front of the saloon disintegrated. He dropped to the sidewalk and crawled under the window, peeking into the saloon. He saw a body about four feet in. Star's shotgun had done its job beautifully. At least ten of the pieces of lead had hit their target: the man's chest. Luke jumped to his feet and charged into the room. He saw one man peeking out from behind the corner of the bar, and caught the image of someone's back running down the hall. He pulled the trigger of his rifle and levered another round into the chamber, firing again so rapidly that it was almost like a single shot. The first bullet hit the man in his left eye, and the second entered his left ear and emerged from the back of his head. He fell backward behind the bar, stone-cold dead, his life blood puddling under him.

Luke took a quick look around and saw Eddie give him the all-clear signal. He headed for the back door and just as he was about to push through, he heard Star's shotgun go off again. Luke heard some of the slugs hit the outside wall. As he stepped outside, he saw the runner lying face down in the dirt, his pistol off to the side. He wasn't moving. Star stood there with the big shotgun at the ready. Luke came over and put his arms around her.

"How did you get back here so fast?" She asked.

"I'm not sure.

"Your grandmother must have helped. She seems to be keeping a very close eye on you...or us."

Luke walked her back over to the sheriff's office, and Macky was waiting.

"Where the hell did you disappear to?" Macky questioned Star. "One second you were there, and the next you were gone. This danged ol' monster dog couldn't even find ya."

"Just had a little business to take care of, sheriff," she responded as she smiled at Luke.

"As close as I can tell that's nine, Macky….Three, maybe four left, if yer count is right. Where do ya s'pose I can find the rest of the gang?"

The sheriff pointed to nowhere in particular, saying, "They been holed up at a small ranch about 4 miles west of town against the side of the mountain. The trail is just past the saw mill 'bout a quarter mile. If ya come at 'um from the back, be very careful. There's a mine shaft about a hundred yards back of the ranch house, and they'll bushwhack ya in a heartbeat. By now they have to know yer comin'."

Luke checked his weapons and kissed Star on the forehead. "I should be back in time for breakfast."

He stepped outside and jumped up on Storm. "Bear, come!" and they headed west at a fast gallop.

Bear had a bounce in his step and a smile on his face, his tongue hanging out and swinging back and forth as he ran. It was still about an hour before sundown, so Luke rode right on past the path into the ranch for about half a mile and headed off into the forest. When he got to where he could see the ranch house, he decided there wasn't enough cover, so he made his way back to the main trail. He rode past the trail into the ranch, going east this time. He passed the saw mill and turned into the trees to his left working his way through the thick brush. Luke dropped the lead rope to the hackamore about fifty yards from the ranch house. He and Bear crawled through the tall green grass until they were about twenty yards from the back corner of the ranch house. They stopped behind a large rock with a scrub brush growing beside it.

He rubbed Bear's head and explained, "We're going to stay right here till a couple hours past dark, then we'll make our move." Bear moved his head from side to side and licked Luke's hand. He understood.

About thirty minutes before dark, a tall dark man with a bushy black beard walked out to the corral and threw some hay over the pine railing for the three horses that ran loose in the enclosure. Luke studied the cowboy, noticing the way he wore his six-gun, and the way he moved very confidently. Of all the men Luke had faced so far, this one seemed the most capable.

"He just might be the leader,…or at least second in charge." Luke thought.

About two hours after sundown, Luke sent Bear around the back of the corral and up to the other corner of the ranch house, using hand signals to get him in place. Luke had made a large bundle of dry grass and weeds and wrapped them around a rock about the size of a wild gourd. He snuck up to the side of the house, pulled himself up to the roof and dropped the bundle of dry grass and weeds down the chimney, hoping the sparks from the fire place would ignite it. Just as Luke was lowering himself back down, a bullet split the log he was holding on to and he let go, dropping to the ground. Even before he landed, he had his sawed-off leveled and he pulled the first trigger, hitting the tall bearded man full in the chest and knocking him backwards to the ground. The man's pistol slipped from his hand. As the second man ran from the back door, obviously not interested in confronting Luke, Bear hit him hard from his left side knocking him off his feet and sending him rolling down the slight grade to the corral. When he stopped rolling, he tried to get up, but Bear was straddling him, teeth bared. Luke walked up, reloaded his shooter and told Bear to heel. He ran to Luke's side and sat beside his right leg. He got a pat of praise on the head and he smiled.

"How many more?" Luke asked.

"Just me and I'm frazzled. I ain't gonna be no trouble. You dun kilt all my men in one day! Who the hell are you anyways?"

"U S Marshal Luke Kash from Taos. And who exactly are you?"

"Maybry. Wil Mabry. This was my folks' place."

"…And you decided it was easier to steal from your friends than to work for it."

"Yeah, somethin' like that."

"Just how long did you think you could keep this up before someone came to put a stop to it?" Luke asked.

"Really didn't give it too much thought." Maybry replied.

"Well, I guess you're a special kind of stupid, aren't ya?"

Maybry just kinda stared at Luke, almost ready to tear up.

"What happens now?" he asked.

"Well, you can do something stupid and die where your lyin', or you can go back to town and get ready to hang. It's kind of up to you. I don't normally take prisoners, so I wouldn't try anything, 'cause Bear's just aching to have a little fun...and if he doesn't kill ya. I sure as hell will. Where's all the ore and loot you been takin' off the miners?"

"At the back of the mine shaft; over there covered up with tarps."

Luke was dumbfounded at how stupid this thirty-something was. He couldn't imagine what might be in the ranch house, but he didn't have time or concern enough to go check. That'll be someone else's job. Luke just wanted to get headed back home, but before he could, he had to escort his prisoner to town to prepare for his fate.

Storm kept up a steady gait as they headed back to town with their prisoner in tow, hands tied out in front. Bear, nipping at his heels, did a good job of making sure he stayed on the straight and narrow. "Sheriff, you need to deputize a couple of folks, and do some house cleaning. That fella in the cell says all the loot is in the mine shaft, and God only knows what's in the ranchhouse. But I suggest you don't wait too long. If word gets out that the gang is gone, there could be a panic headed out there to get their stuff back."

"I have just the right boys for the job; not gun hands, but good honest folks,"Macky offered.

Luke replied, "Good! Go get 'um moving. Me and Star are gonna go wake up the cook at the cafe, then head back to camp. I'll leave it up to you to get the miners together for a meeting in the saloon at 9AM. I'll see ya there."

The mules were fine and the roan was standing between them…just one of the team. Luke opened the bottle of brandy and poured a generous portion in their tin cups as they sat back on the bed inside their lodge-on-wheels.

"That's wonderful! What is it?" Star marvelled.

"Just a little something from a placed called Paris. That's somewhere over in France."

Luke was too tired to make sense of it all. He took one long pull and swallowed the contents of his cup, then fell straight to sleep, his head landing on Star's lap.

The next morning, about thirty minutes before daylight, Luke was sitting in the river letting the cold water run over his long blond hair. Bear was standing by his side and Storm was walking around in the water. It felt amazing to all three. After about ten minutes, he got up and walked, naked, back to the lodge. He got dressed and prepared to meet the day. By 7AM, he and Morning Star were back in the little cafe at the same table as the night before. They ate ham and eggs and hot biscuits with wild berry preserves, and cup after cup of hot coffee.

Luke told Star to eat up, "It'll be a while 'til the evening meal."

The cook came out and asked Luke if he could do anything for the couple and Luke handed him a $20 gold piece and thanked him for his good service and food.

"Marshal, uhh I can't make change for this!"

"You don't need to, Cookie. Just have the coffee hot the next time were through town."

"I sure will, Marshal, and the next time yer here, it's on me."

Luke smiled to himself and thought, "Who said money can't buy friends, at least for a while?"

Luke met with the miners and the sheriff and explained that they needed to form an association and how it would benefit everyone. He could tell they thought it would be a good idea. He tossed Eddie, the barkeep, a $50 gold piece and told him to keep the good stuff coming 'til it ran out.

"Oh yeah, and give the sheriff another bottle of that brandy." He tossed Eddie another gold coin and headed out to check the team and to meet Star, Bear and Storm.

CHAPTER 6

They headed east out of Silver City about ten in the morning and kept to the trail through the South end of the Mimbres Mountains. The going was slow heading down hill and Luke rode the brake to keep the wagons from pushing the mules. He stopped every hour or so to check the mules' hooves for rocks and give them water. They made good time considering. Bear spent a lot of time between Luke and Star on the wagon seat, and that was fine with them.

They spent that night in the cool pines by a rushing stream. Luke caught fish and Bear brought a pheasant to the party while the stock grazed on sweet green grass and fresh mountain water. Star gathered some kind of vegetables that Luke wasn't familiar with, and cooked them in bacon grease in the cast iron pot. They laid the fish and bird over the flames on the grate that Gunther had made. Star broke out her special seasonings, and everything was amazing. Luke was starting to relax. He absolutely loved being outdoors and on the trail with a good woman, a great horse and a fine dog. "What else could a man ask for?" Luke thought to himself. "How 'bout a warm bed and a roof over your head?" and he realized that he had that as well.

After Star had finished cleaning camp and Bear had eaten his fill, Luke made his way into the lodge and poured two cups of brandy. Star came in after bathing in the stream and stood in front of Luke letting her buckskin dress fall to the floor.

"Are you man enough for this?" she teased.

"What do you think?"

The next morning at sunup Luke was still asleep. He woke to some unfamiliar sounds and looked out the window on the starboard side of the wagon. Star was standing by the fire with a cast-iron skillet in her hand scraping it with a wooden spoon, just loud enough for Luke to hear.

"What's that noise?" he shouted.

"Your morning wake-up call, Mr US Marshal. Sooo… now that you don't have a real job to go to, you think you can just lay around all day? she taunted playfully.

"I'll show you lying around!" He jumped down from the wagon and ran to her. They embraced and he cradled her in his arms. While she thought she was being romanced, in one swift move, Luke scooped her up, walked into the stream and dropped her. She came up from the cold water snorting and spitting, trying to find an indian word that would tell Luke what she thought of him at that very moment. Try as she might, the indian language didn't have anything that harsh.

"You shit!" she exploded, half laughing.

Luke could see the smile on her face as well as the fire in her eyes. He knew he would pay for it later. "…completely worth it," he thought to himself.

After about an hour, her buckskin dress had begun to shrink from the water and Luke thought she looked even more amazing than before.

"How was that possible?" Luke marvelled. They continued on down the mountain and by mid-afternoon they reached the Rio Grande River. Luke turned the team north and wrapped the reins loosely around the brake handle and let the team find their own pace. They always traveled faster than Luke thought was possible. The two mules loved to pull in tandem and they loved being on the trail, too.

About four in the afternoon, Luke found a place along the river that had large cottonwood trees that he pulled the wagons up under for shelter. That night around ten, Luke heard the first sign of thunder crashing in from the northwest while it was still ten or twelve miles away. He went outside and dropped the roll-down shelter that Gunther had designed. He brought the mules, the big gray, the roan and Storm up under the cover. After a quick look around, he and Bear went back inside and he poured some brandy for him and Star.

"Be sure and remind me to order three or four cases of this when we get back to Taos."

"Don't you worry about that. This is absolutely the best firewater ever, and if we run out you're gonna have one pissed-off indian princess on your hands.

"Yes, my darling, I know you'll never let me forget that you are the daughter of the chief of the Ute nation."

CHAPTER 7

They followed the river for the next two days and ended up back at the village where the old women had their pots cooking. Luke pulled the wagons up as close to the mud huts as possible and unhitched the team. By the time he had them grazing, two old ladies showed up with a board that had burritos piled high on it. They handed it to Luke and giggled. It looked like they had new dresses and bandanas around their heads, and they were in a much better frame of mind than the last time Luke and Star were here. He didn't try to pay them for the food; he knew it would only insult them and he truly did not want to do that.

The next morning, an hour before sunup, Luke had the team hitched. He and Star had already had their meal and they were moving onto the trail along the river. Luke had a feeling that they were being watched; he had felt it since early the day before. As the sun hit the mountain Luke caught a glimpse of a half-dozen indians on the horizon and he smiled.

He looked at Star, "Looks like our protectors are on the job."

"Yeah, I know. I saw them yesterday morning"

"Why didn't you say something?"

"What? Yer an indian...well kind-of. I thought you knew."

Luke mumbled something in the Ute dialect that referred to a lowly wife and her role in life, and he caught a fist in the ribs.

"You better watch yer mouth paleface. I'll have my red brothers out there relieve you of that pretty golden hair. Boy...a little knowledge and some cash and you forget your station in life."

She hit him in the ribs again this time almost taking his breath away.

"OK, OK. I give! Stop beating on me. I have to take care of you and I can't do it if I'm all beat to pieces."

"Take care of me? Are you serious? Who pulled your butt out of the fire more than once this last week?"

"You did, dear."

Bear barked his agreement and they both laughed.

They pulled up into the yard of their ranch about three in the afternoon. Marshal Brady Simms was sitting on the front porch in one of the rocking chairs, big smile on his face.

"You kids about through with yer vacationin' so we can get back to work?"

Luke gave him a look, "If that was a vacation, I don't want to see what work is like around here." They both grinned.

"You wanna head up Colorado way after ya get a couple a days rest," the Marshal asked.

Luke didn't need to think about it, "Sure, Brady, I've got some business in Denver I need to wrap up, and we could stand to see our families for a day or two."

Star came out with two glasses of brandy and handed them to the men. Brady took a sniff and then a swallow and his eyes lit up.

"Damn son, that's some mighty fine sippin' right there. By the way, that was some really fine marshalin' up there in Silver. What the hell did you do, just walk into town and shoot every one you saw? How many men did you bury in the last two weeks?"

"Including the Mexican bandidos? Luke asked.

"The what?...Yeah!"

"There was a bunch of 'em that hit us about four days out, but some of my brothers were traveling with us and those bandits got quite a surprise.

"Damn son, yer kinda like one of them new magnets when it comes to bad men, ain't cha?"

"Well, I guess so, but isn't that what you hired me for?"

"Yeah, I guess it is." Brady stood and grabbed the reins of his horse and stepped aboard. "By the way, one hell of a job, Marshal Kash."

He turned his horse around and headed down the hill. As great as the bed in the cabin on wheels was, it didn't compare to the big feather bed upstairs in their home. Luke slept until thirty minutes after sunup and when he rolled over, he found Star right there as well. He patted her bottom and the next thing you know…well, you know.

Luke dressed leisurely in brown denim jeans, a flannel shirt and some soft leather boots. Heading down stairs, he realized someone had made a pot of coffee. Luke was confused.

"Oh, that little wench."

He poured himself a cup and walked outside. One of the ranch hands walked by and Luke asked him to bring Storm out. He finished his coffee and left the cup on the arm of the rocking chair. He climbed up on Storm and headed down the hill to visit with Teddy and Becky Moore at the butcher shop. Luke hadn't reached the stream when he got a whiff of fresh baking bread coming through the air. He reined Storm up behind the shop by the walk-in smoker and dropped the hackamore lead to the ground. He walked up and knocked on the back door.

"Come on in, Luke," Becky's voice came through wooden door. She greeted him with a steaming cup of coffee and a plate of hot rolls with a big scoop of fresh butter. "Have a seat boss," she said, giving him a big hug.

"Where's Teddy?" Luke asked. "…and does everyone in town know I'm back?"

"I'd be very surprised if they didn't; you're their hero…and Teddy's making a delivery over to the café. He should be back soon."

"How's business, Beck? he asked.

"Really good, but not as good as yours from what I hear."

"Don't believe every thing you hear."

"Well, it must be true or you wouldn't be back, and in one piece too."

Luke just smiled and sipped his coffee, spreading peach preserves on a roll. "It doesn't get much better than this," he thought to himself.

Teddy walked through the door with a big smile on his face. "Hey Boss! How was yer trip?"

"That's partner to you, and it was fine but it's good to be home for a couple of days. Brady's got us heading north in a day or two. How are things with you, Luke asked."

"You want to see the books?"

"Nah. I don't need to see any books; your word's good 'nuff for me. Besides, I got Brady keepin' an eye on you." They all laughed.

They talked for an hour or so until Luke saw Brady ride by. He excused himself and invited them for dinner that evening as he walked out back to get Storm. He rode around behind the livery and caught a glimpse of Gunther. "How ya doin', my friend? I have a meeting with the marshal but I'll be back with you before the end of the day. By the way, there's a real nice strawberry roan and some weapons up at the ranch if you could pick them up. And tell my friend Miguel I look forward to seeing him."

Marshal Brady Simms was making a pot of coffee when Luke walked in.

"Mornin' son. How ya doin'? Did ya get some rest?"

"Yeah, I did. I stayed in the sack 'til after sunrise. Been doin' that more and more lately."

"Well, I guess when yer a gentleman rancher and a man of leisure you can do that," and he smiled at Luke.

"When does the leisure kick in? Luke joked.

"Luke, I have some issues in Denver that should be right up yer alley. One of the ranchers is buying up mortgages from the banks and the forcing the owners to pay them off, or get out. I have some information that he is holding stolen cattle so he can control the price of beef in Colorado," Brady explained.

"I need to spend a few days with my grandparents, but it's just a short ride over to Denver from the village, so this should work out fine. I have a few more business meetings than I expected, so if it's okay with you, I'll leave on Friday instead of the day after tomorrow."

"This has been going on for a time, so another couple of days ain't gonna make any difference."

Luke took all the notes and information and put them in his pouch. He told the marshal to let him know if he needed him before they left on Friday morning.

"Oh yeah, and dinner's at seven," he remembered.

"I'll be there," Brady said with a smile.

Luke rode down the main street of Taos, New Mexico and thought, "How did a young half-breed get to be the biggest land owner in the area in just five short years?" He remembered like it was yesterday…leading his herd of farm animals up the trail with Storm hitched to the ox cart, and the old dog, Skeeter, keeping the stock together, not knowing where they were going to spend the night or where their next meal was coming from.

He saw old Hank, the street cleaner, and rode over by him. "How you doin', Hank?"

"Doin' purdy well, Marshal, thanks fer askin'. Luke flipped him a $10 gold piece.

A wagon coming up the muddy street broke Luke's train of thought. It was Harvy and Molly Brown. He had known them ever since he moved to town. They were some of his best customers from the days when he delivered for Ma and Papa Johansen's butcher shop. Their wagon was loaded with some household goods and a few personal items, but not much for traveling.

"Hey Harvy, where you headed? Luke inquired.

"We're movin' on. The bank gonna take the ranch in a week or so 'cause we're so far behind there ain't nothin' we can do 'bout it. Somebody's been makin' the price of beef go down to where it cost us money to sell a head."

"Well, where ya headed?"

"East, I guess. Maybe get some work with the railroad if I'm lucky."

"Have you got traveling money?" Luke asked."

"Got about $3, but we'll do alright," he replied.

Luke thought for a minute, "When did you say the bank was going to take the ranch?"

"Next week. Don't rightly know which day…don't matter much."

"Harvy, would you follow me over to the bank for a few minutes?" Luke suggested.

"Yeah, I guess, few minutes ain't gonna make much difference. Don't gotta be no place particular." Molly looked at Luke with tears in her eyes and tried to smile, to no avail. It almost broke Luke's heart.

The bank manager, Mr. Weathers, who Luke suspected was also the owner, was sitting at his desk. When he saw Luke, he jumped to his feet almost tripping over himself to shake his hand.

"Mr. Kash, how wonderful to see you! How can I be of service to you?"

"I understand the bank is taking Harvy's ranch for back payments. Is that right?"

"Umm, yes sir, that is correct." Mr. Weathers affirmed.

"When and how much does he owe? Uhh, next Tuesday, and it would take about…umm…exactly $208 to get current.

"How much is the loan on the ranch?" Luke demanded, casually leaning back in his chair.

"Yes sir, let me…uhh…let me check here." He fumbled through a very large ledger on his desk while Luke sat and waited. Harvy stood nervously beside him, hat in hand.

"Umm, the balance on the property is…seven thousand three hundred dollars," Mr. Weathers reluctantly confirmed.

"I would like to buy this property from Harvy," Luke declared. "Is that alright with you Harv?" Luke smiled, turning to Harvy.

"Uhh, yeah…that's fine with me," Harvy replied, only half believing what was happening.

"How much do you want for the ranch, buddy?" Luke asked Harvy.

"Well, I dunno know; maybe a couple hundred dollars I guess."

"Mr. Weathers, would you please give Harvy here a hundred dollars cash traveling money, and make him a check for four hundred so he can deposit it when he gets where he is going?" Luke saw the disappointment in the banker's face. He new he had just lost a great opportunity to gain some property.

"When you get Harvy fixed up here, transfer the money from my account to pay off the ranch and I'll be by later today to sign the papers and get the title," Luke instructed.

"Yes sir, Mr Kash. I'll have them ready after lunch." The banker was almost in tears.

Luke shook Harvy's hand and wished him safe travels. He walked outside and found Molly still sitting in the wagon. He climbed up and sat beside her on the wagon seat, put his arms around her and said, "I have a feeling things are gonna be fine, so dry those eyes," and he kissed her forehead.

Bear barked loudly. Luke rode down to the livery and found Gunther working on some horseshoes for a large draft horse. Gunther came over and they shook hands and hugged, man-style.

"How's business?" Luke asked him.

"It's good, and the fact that I don't have a payment every month makes the bottom line look even better. I'll never be able to repay you."

"Don't worry about it," Luke responded warmly. "How is our little gun-and-pony show coming along?"

"Really good! You keep bringin' 'em in, and I'll keep sellin' 'em,"Gunther exclaimed.

"I'll be leaving for the north on Friday. Will you check the mules and Star's gray before we hit the trail?"

"Sure will."Gunther responded.

"Is Miguel in the gunshop?"

"Yeah, he's very excited to see you. I'll go over Storm while yer visitin' with him."

"Thanks, Gunther, yer a good friend." Luke said.

"Leave me that ugly ol' knife too, and I'll put an edge on it while yer with Miguel." Luke hated to part with the magical weapon. It had never been out of reach since Gunther presented it to him four years ago.

Miguel was at his workbench and had parts of a gun spread everywhere. When he heard Luke enter, his eyes lit up and he jumped to his feet. They shook hands and hugged.

"Meester Luke, my good friend, how are you? Let me have your weapons so I can check them before you leave." Luke removed his sawed-off shotgun from the holster and unloaded it. He laid it on Miguel's workbench and did the same with his Colt PeaceMaker. Miguel went right to work as Luke watched and marvelled at his expertise. He was truly a master gunsmith.

"Miguel, how is your lovely wife?"

"Oh, Meester Luke, she works very hard washing clothes for the peoples in the town. She is getting older and starting to get more tired."

"Yes, I know, she is a fine woman. I have a proposition for you, my friend," Luke paused. "…Do you know the Brown ranch just out of town?"

"Yes, Meester Luke, I know it well."

"I bought it and we are going to put livestock on it for the butcher shop. I was hoping you might be interested in living there and you and your wife could oversee the property. There's a large wood cabin out back where you could tan the hides and sell them to Gunther."

Miguel wasn't exactly sure what Luke was saying, but he listened. "How mush do I have to pay you to live there? Miguel questioned.

Luke knew that was coming. "I was going to pay you a hundred dollars a month to watch over things."

"You are going to give me money to live at your ranch?"

"Yeah. Is that alright with you?…And your wife can take it a little easier and maybe help you tan the hides."

"Oh my! She will be so please. A house with a room to sleep in and a kitchen to cook. Oh thank you, Meester Luke!"

"Go to the mercantile and get whatever you need to make it a home. I'll tell Buck Jones to expect you."

Luke went back outside and Gunther had Storm's shoes tightened and was feeding him juicy red apples. The big horse was in heaven. Luke told Gunther about the plans for Miguel and that he would be providing him with hides for the shop from the ranch from now on. Gunther just smiled and thought to himself, "What a special man and a great friend."

Luke walked next door and had a meal with Teddy. He told him about the ranch and that Miguel and his wife would be living there. They discussed buying butchering stock and building a herd. "When the price of beef goes down, buy whatever you think we need and put them on the ranch. We'll be better suited to make a little more profit when prices are low."

Teddy liked the idea and they shook hands. Just as Luke was getting ready to leave, four riders tied up to the hitchin' post outside the butcher shop.

"That's Becky's pa and his foreman." Becky stepped out on the boardwalk and greeted her father.

"Hi Daddy! What are you doin' in Taos?"

"Came to take you home gal. You got no business workin' in a greasy ol' place like this. Yer my daughter! Get yer things together, we're goin home!"

"Sorry Daddy. This is our home and this is our business, and you ran us off without a thing, if you remember."

"I don't care 'bout that, just get yer belongin's and let's get outta here."

"I'm exactly where I want to be, Daddy, and I'm not going anywhere."

Luke and Teddy walked out the door and stood on the sidewalk beside Becky. Teddy spoke up, "Becky's my wife and this is our home, and we're stayin' right here; so you better leave before there's trouble."

"Don't threaten me ya some bitch, I'll blow yer god damn head off!"

Luke spoke up, "I wouldn't go talkin' like that, mister. I don't like citizens being threatened in my town."

"And just who the hell are you, ya young pup? Ya better get outta my way 'fore I put a slug in yer young ass."

Becky cried out, "Daddy, that's Luke Kash, U.S.Marshal, and I wouldn't brace him if I were you!"

The rancher's eyes opened wide at the name. "Kash huh?" He calmed.

Luke said, "Mister, if you don't do exactly as I say and you try something stupid, the first thing I'm going to do is blow yer head off. Then, I'm going to assume those three are gonna follow yer lead, so I'm gonna put a bullet in them as well. What do ya say?"

Bear was at his right thigh and he growled very loudly.

"Just calm down young fella, we don't want no problems."

"You're welcome to come in and order some coffee and a bite if you can behave yourself," Becky invited.

"Leave yer shooters hanging on your saddles and don't make me come back here," Luke informed the riders.

Becky told her father that Luke was their business partner, and that life was good, and that was that. She handed him a bill for seven dollars. He threw a $20 gold piece on the table and the three men followed him outside. They mounted up and rode off to the south.

Luke took the title to the Brown ranch and put it in his pouch, shook Mr. Weather's frail hand and headed Storm and Bear toward home. A thought hit him and he reined Storm up in front of the Welcome Inn. Harvy Vaughn, the owner and Luke's tenant, saw him coming and ran to the back to draw an ice cold beer the way Luke liked it.

"Hey Harvy, how have you been?" He handed Luke the glass of beer and reached to shake his hand.

"It's been really quiet around here since you left. Sure could use some new shade on the windows." Luke grinned.

"Hey Harvy, you got any of that French brandy?"

"Funny you should ask, a peddler came by yesterday and left a bottle. Said if it didn't sell, he'd pick it up next trip through."

"I'll take it off yer hands," and he tossed a $10 gold piece on the bar. "Is that enough?"

"You bet. Let me get yer change!"

"Keep it," Luke finished his beer and headed home.

Morning Star had one of the ranch hand's wives come up to help her with some dishes she wasn't familiar with. Luke had become very fond of green chile stew, flour tortillas and fried beans, and she wanted to surprise him. That evening at dinner, Luke announced to everyone that he'd bought the Brown spread and the plans that he and Teddy had. Star still found it hard to imagine how wealthy they really were.

Bowls of chile verde, rice, beans cooked in pork fat, fresh tortillas…Luke was in heaven. He hired the lady in the kitchen to be their full-time cook. Then she brought out a delicious flan, and Luke gave her a raise on the spot. He could only think of one thing that could make this night better…Luke broke out the new bottle of brandy and they all enjoyed it sitting on the wooden porch in the rocking chairs with the cool breeze coming up from the valley. God, life was good.

CHAPTER 8

Friday morning the two ranch hands were up at 4AM loading supplies in the ox-cart. Luke wasn't far behind, checking the mules and Storm and Star's gray. Bear was running around barking and directing the ranch hands. He was ready to get on the trail. An hour before sunup they headed down the trail to town, Luke and Star on the padded seat of their mobile lodge. The gray was tied to the back of the ox cart and Storm and Bear were running loose to the side of the wagon. Although they had only been back in town a few days, Luke was more than ready to see his grandparents and Star felt the same about her family.

The trail from Taos north was just as beautiful as they remembered. The streams and tall pines, the wild life and the oak trees were incredible. The meadows that Bear and Storm would frolic through made Star and Luke smile. Life really was spectacular. Two days later in the afternoon they rode into the Ute village. Luke could smell the cook fires and see the people gathered.

"Well, looks like my grandmother, the witch, has been at it again."

Star agreed. They had no idea how she did what she did, but it was truly amazing.

That evening the family gathered around the cook fires: Morning Star's father, the chief of the Utes, her mother and Luke's grandmother, the Shaman, and his Grandfather, Charging Buffalo. They feasted on venison, elk, wild pig and rainbow trout, squaw bread with wild honey and lots of nuts and fresh berries. Bear enjoyed the spoils as well. They listened while Star told of the exploits of her husband, and Luke reiterated the times Star had saved his life and how invaluable she was to him. She smiled and kissed his hand. The indians stared at them, not used to seeing this kind of public display of affection.

After dinner, Yellow Eagle, Luke's young friend, joined their gathering. He had shot up at least three inches since Luke's last visit, when he would follow Luke around like a young puppy trying to get to the tit. Even though he was no longer a young indian boy, he was still in awe of the great Walks With Bears. Luke told Yellow Eagle that after he returned from Denver, the two of them would round up some wild horses.

Later that evening, Luke's grandmother gave him the usual new set of buckskins and two pair of moccasins, and a beautiful new soft deerskin dress decorated with beads and turquoise for Star. "How did she know the sizes?" he thought. "They always fit perfectly, very strange."

Luke offered to let Morning Star stay in the village while he went to Denver, but she would not hear of it. He had learned it was pointless to argue with her.

The next morning before sunrise, Yellow Eagle was outside their lodge with the mules. Luke already had the ox-cart secured and everything in the wagon in its place. They were off, heading northeast toward Denver.

The trail was narrow and grown over in some places, mostly used by indian ponies, some pulling traverses with game and trading supplies. Every few hours Luke would climb aboard Storm and ride ahead, along with Bear, for several miles checking out the change in landscape and the signs along the trail, looking for places to camp and just getting a feel for the new country in general. The maps that his boss, Marshal Brady Simms, furnished him were reasonably accurate, although some stretches were very vague. Luke would have to use his experience and judgment. Luckily his instincts and the training his father had instilled in him proved to be invaluable. They had just made camp along a fast-running spring late afternoon on the second day when Bear came to his side and growled, then moved away about ten feet looking up the trail. Luke walked up and crouched beside him.

"Go see," and the huge dog ran off to the west into the forest and disappeared into the tall pines and evergreen brush. Luke motioned to Star and she grabbed the 12-gauge shotgun that lately was always within reach. She cracked the breech and checked both barrels, putting the strap of the pouch full of shells over her head and right shoulder so it hung and rested on her left hip. A few minutes later, Bear snuck back into camp with blood dripping from his mouth. Luke checked him over and he was fine; in fact, his tail was wagging. He grunted and moved back to the perimeter of the camp and looked back at Luke. Luke signaled Star to take cover, then he sent Bear off to the west again. He moved off to the east and down into the stream, hugging the bank as he waded through the fast-running icy water. About fifty yards upstream he saw the first of the braves moving stealthily downstream about five or six yards away from the water. He took a deep breath and slid beneath the water, pulling himself upstream using the large stones on the river bottom. When his instincts told him he was in position, he reached down and removed his skinning knife from the legging of his right moccasin, grabbed it by the blade and emerged from the frigid water. He focused his eyes and threw the knife. The razor-sharp blade buried deep in the indian's chest and he fell to the ground, moved his legs slightly a couple of times then began his journey to the happy hunting ground. Luke crawled out of the water and retrieved his knife from the red man's chest, wiping the blade clean on the indian's leather chaps. He noticed the quality of the bow the dead man had in his possession, and he took the quiver full of arrows and the weapon and moved off into the trees. He had only moved a few paces when he heard a blood-curdling scream. He knew that Bear had taken another soul and sent it on its way to the great spirit. The noise caused an indian about ten yards up ahead to start and turn to see where the sound was coming from. He exposed his torso just long enough for Luke to place an arrow under his left armpit. It tore through the skin and muscle and broke two ribs as it lodged in his heart. The indian slumped to the earth, face down on the forest floor. He took one last breath and Luke saw his spirit drift off to to join his fellow warriors.

"How is that possible?" he thought. "Grandma, are you out there?"

Bear came bouncing up to him, and Luke knew that the danger was past and that all the attackers were dead. Luke checked all the bodies for anything he and Gunther could sell but found little of value. A couple of hand-made knives and the bow and arrows were the only things he considered to be worth saving. He checked the trail and found that one of the braves had escaped and was headed north as fast as his worn-out horse could carry him. Bear gathered the indians' ponies and led them back to camp for Luke's inspection. They were small and old and not worth dragging to Denver and back, so Luke tied a rope between two trees and tethered the ponies overnight. He would release them in the morning.

Luke felt something and realized it was his grandmother telling him to take cover. In the last few weeks he had been getting more and more impressions. Visions? Messages? Whatever they were, he wasn't exactly sure, but he was definitely grateful for the help.

"There's a storm coming, my son. Take cover." He dropped the shelter on the east side of the wagon and brought the mules and their two horses under the cover. He went inside to change into his new dry buckskins and moccasins. He found that Star had a fire in the cast-iron stove and was getting ready to cook. The first thing she did was come to Luke and hug him. She was surprised to find that his skin was not cold at all. She looked at him strangely and he just shrugged….

"Grandmother, I guess."

Star soon had coffee brewing and a pot of potatoes, carrots and dried beef boiling on the small stove. Normally, Luke would have Bear sleep under the wagon after an attack for security, but grandma didn't tell him about anything but the storm. And indians don't like being wet any more than anyone else. The storm came from the west and hit hard, but Luke and Star were high and dry; in fact, Star loved stormy weather…the rougher the better. She stayed awake for an hour or more enjoying the storm. Luke fell right off to sleep. Killing hostiles is exhausting work.

Sometime in the middle of the night, Luke woke and sat straight up in bed.

"Good evening, my love," Morning Star greeted. "What can I do for you?"

He smiled and they made love…and love…and luv.

Daylight brought a bright sunny day. They ate a hearty breakfast of cornmeal mush, berries, nuts and hot coffee, and Luke estimated that a hard days ride would put them in or around Denver. The day was uneventful and they saw the rooftops of Denver in the distance by late afternoon. Luke kept on going until he found a perfect spot by the river to make camp, then he and Bear made the short trek into town. They pulled up in front of the sheriff's office. He dropped the hackamore to the ground and Storm bellied up to the water trough and drank. Luke walked into the sheriff's office with Bear at his heels. Sheriff Gaylord Rose almost jumped out of his skin when he looked up and saw the giant dog sitting at Luke's side.

"You must be Marshal Kash. I didn't know exactly when to expect you, but everyone in the country has heard about yer dog."

They shook hands and Luke asked him some questions. He found out that the marshal that was assigned to Denver had been ambushed a week or so back.

"He knew you were comin' but them bad hombres got to him first." Luke was really sorry but couldn't dwell on it.

"Do you have his badge and belongings, Sheriff?"

"Yeah, I do," and he dug the badge and holstered colt out of his desk drawer.

"Anything else?" Luke asked.

"Nah, I'm afraid the outlaws got the rest. I do have his horse and rig over at the livery if ya want 'um."

"Just make sure his horse is well taken care of and I'll pick it up as I'm leaving town."

"Yes sir, Marshal, nothin' but the best for the US Marshals."

Luke looked the old man hard into his eyes. He wanted to make sure he was on the right side of his badge. He decided that he could be trusted and asked, "Sheriff, tell me, how many deputies do you have?"

"I got three that are in one piece, a couple more that got bullet holes in 'um, buried one of my best ones yesterday."

"Sorry about that, Sheriff. I guess it's about time we put these troublemakers where they belong."

"I understand you don't take prisoners. Is that right?"

"Well, most of the time I don't have any choice. Bad guys seem to want to brace me. Guess I don't look like much of a gun fighter."

"Just lookin at that monster at yer side is enough to make me drop my shooter."

"Yeah, I guess he is pretty intimidating, but he's really a lover, unless you rile him or make a move against his family."

"How many fighters did you bring with you?" the sheriff asked.

"Well, I've got Bear here and my wife back at our camp."

The sheriff's jaw dropped. "That's all?" he asked.

"As close as I can tell, there's only one problem here, right? And we got yer deputies. That makes a pretty nice little posse if ya ask me."

"I guess yer right," the sheriff shook his head.

"Have yer men meet me here at sunup and we'll lay this plan out and put an end to this craziness."

The sheriff said, "I'll drink to that. Will ya join me?"

"Sure. I've got a little dust in my gullet, so why not?"

As they walked across the street to the saloon, Luke asked if there was anything he should be aware of before they entered.

"No, we purdy much keep them out of town. My boys keep a 24-hour watch from top of the bank building."

"Yeah," Luke replied, "I saw him as I rode in."

"Yer good," the old lawman said as they entered.

The next morning at sunup, Luke, Star and Bear all moved up to the hitching post outside the sheriff's office and went inside. The sheriff had a large coffee pot on the cast-iron stove and he began to pour tin cups for his guests. Luke introduced Morning Star to the deputies and the sheriff. They all looked a little apprehensive, as she was young, slight and beautiful. But the long-barrel 12-gauge shotgun slung over her shoulder did make her look a little bigger.

Luke began, "I did some scouting around last night, and it looks to me like there's about ten or twelve, not counting the boss. Does that sound about right?"

One of the deputies spoke up, "Yeah Marshal, that's exactly right. There's twelve shooters and the boss, Raymond George. He stays in the ranch house for the most part; haven't seen him but once or twice since this whole thing started. So what's yer plan, Marshal?" the young deputy asked.

"Well, I guess I'll go introduce myself to the good Mr. George."

All but Star stood there with their mouths agape. She had a grin.

"Are you sure that's a good idea, Marshal? They plug folks on sight."

"Well, I guess I'll have to turn sideways."

They looked at him confused. "Smaller target," Luke said and smiled, and they got the joke and chuckled as well.

Luke made sure the deputies had Winchesters and a full complement of ammunition for their rifles and hand guns. Luke hadn't been paying much attention to the days, and it finally dawned on him that it was Sunday.

"I doubt they'll be in church," he said out loud, and everyone laughed.

They rode out of town and Luke explained the rest of his plan as they headed in the direction of the George ranch. Luke pulled them up about three hundred and fifty yards from the ranch house.

"Hey Marshal. We can't hit anything from here. Hell, I can just barely see the house from here!"

"Don't worry," and Luke pulled his 52-caliber Sharps rifle, broke it open and checked the load. He jumped down from Storm and dropped the rein, and walked up to a large boulder that gave him a direct view of the ranch.

"Whatever you do, don't fire until you hear my third shot. And if no one is running out of the house or the other shack, don't shoot."

The tree line was about twenty to twenty-five yards from the house on both sides, Luke placed the first deputy even with the ranch house on the left side so he could see its back door and the front and only door of the bunk house. The second he placed in the same position on the right side. The third claimed to be the best shot of the lot, so Luke put him up the mountain higher than the rest, but not far enough that his Winchester would be ineffective inside the 200-yard maximum range. He could see every angle of the ranch house from there. Luke had marked each position with a piece of red cloth under a rock the night before while he and Bear did their scouting so the deputies could find exactly the spot that he wanted them to take up. He had Star take a position about twenty yards off to the right so she could cover him while he made his way down the mountain after he laid his Sharps down.

When Luke saw that everyone was in the exact spot he had for them, he took two more bullets from his pouch and held them between his third and fourth, and fourth and fifth fingers on his left hand. He put the long rifle on top of his ammo pouch that was laying on the boulder that Luke had picked out for himself. He pulled it to his shoulder and sighted it in on the porch lamp. He figured it to be about 380 yards, just a comfortable shot for the Sharps buffalo gun. He raised his hand and every one signaled in turn that they were ready. Luke pulled the hammer back and looked down the barrel. He saw movement through the window at the front of the house and he fired. The worn curtains moved and the figure disappeared. There was no doubt in his mind that high-grade bullet found its target. He broke the breach of the big gun and loaded another 52-caliber round and took close aim. Sighting down the barrel through the window on the other side of the front door, he could see a lantern he assumed was on a table. He fired. The lantern exploded and fire spread almost instantly. The dry wood of the ranch house went up like kindling. Luke could see it spreading so fast no one would have a chance to put it out. The front door opened and a man with a Winchester came out firing frantically in all directions. With his last round loaded, Luke took aim and put a bullet in his left eye and his head exploded like someone dropping a melon from a roof. The man flew backward and his lifeless body slammed against the log siding of the farmhouse. Luke leaned his long gun against the boulder, slipped the strap of the ammo pouch over his head, and grabbed his Winchester. He ran as fast as he could, jumping over bushes and fallen logs and rocks to get beside Star. She heard him coming but she never took her eyes off her target. Luke was about ten yards from Star when he heard the 12-gauge explode. He looked at the front of the house and saw another figure fall to the porch and shudder a few times, left lying dead in a pool of his own blood. He slid up beside her and she smiled at him as he laid his hand on her shoulder. Bear came up behind and stuck his big head between them.

The rifleman up the mountain was the second to shoot when he saw someone break the rear window of the bunkhouse. He fired as the hombre was half-way out and left him dead, hanging over the sill with a 44.40 in his chest. The ranch house was being engulfed in flames. Luke left Star and moved down the hill closer to the rear of the house since he knew anyone left inside would have to come out the back. He signaled the deputy on the west side to move towards the back of the property to keep whoever was left alive in a cross fire. Two men ran out the front of the bunkhouse, guns blazing, but they had no idea where their attackers were so their shots went wild. The deputy on the left and the one on the right each squeezed the trigger simultaneously and the two saddle tramps fell to the ground almost as one.

"That's six," Luke thought to himself and continued down the hill.

He looked around for Bear, but he was nowhere in sight. Then he saw him come around the west side of the building and go in the back door. "Bear!" he shouted, but the sound of the fire and the confusion kept the dog from hearing.

Two seconds later, Luke heard shots from inside the house and he thought he heard Bear cry out, but he couldn't be sure. He ran to the back door just as Bear was dragging a man out by the collar of his corduroy coat. The man was screaming and flailing his arms trying to get away from the big dog, to no avail. Bear dragged him out to a grassy area about ten feet away. He saw Luke and released the man. Bear looked Luke in the eyes, then he collapsed.

Luke said to the rancher, "Make a move so I can blow yer head off! Please!"

That's when he noticed the blood under Bear's left shoulder. He ran to his dog and picked him up, cradling him in his arms. Luke noticed warm blood in his left hand coming from a hole in front of Bear's right shoulder. He lifted the almost two-hundred-pound animal like he was a feather, and whistled for Storm. The big horse came running down the road to the ranch house.

He said to Star and the closest deputy, "I don't know how many are left, but round them up; and if they give you any problem at all, shoot them!"

Storm bent down on his front knees and Luke straddled him with Bear in his arms. They ran like the wind, the great horse knew that his best friend was in danger and he covered the four miles in record time. Luke guided the horse with his knees and Storm slid to a stop in front of the doctor's office. The sign read, "Dr. C. Shaw, Surgery and Dentistry and General Heath Care."

Luke kicked the door and it almost came off the hinges. He walked straight through the office into the back room and laid Bear on the operating table. Doc Shaw followed right behind him.

"Hey! What the hell do ya think yer doin'? I ain't no vet!"

"You'd better learn to be one in the next couple of seconds or you'll never have to worry about what kind of doctor you are from now on."

"What do ya mean, ya son of a bitch?"

"That's Marshal son of a bitch to you and you're wasting time."

The doc saw the badge hanging around Luke's neck, saw the very big man with the long blond hair and the huge dog, and put two and two together. All his bravery went right out the window.

"Here! Hold this cloth over his muzzle," and Luke did. The doc poured a few drops of some clear liquid on the cloth and Bear started breathing easier. The doctor probed in both wounds and stuffed patches soaked in alcohol in the front and exit holes.

"Well Marshal, the good news is the bullet went clear through without hittin' any vitals. If ya didn't shake all the blood out of him on the way in, he may have a chance. Luke looked down at his buckskins and saw that he was covered with blood from head to toe.

"Yeah, I see what you mean. Sorry I was so rough on you Doc, but this is a very special animal and I don't plan on losing him."

"If I can keep him quiet for a couple of days he should be okay."

"What can I do to help?"

"Just go on about yer business and I'll hunt ya down if I need to."

Luke rubbed the big dog's head then walked out the door and headed back to the ranch. About half-way there he saw riders coming his way: the deputies, Star and three men in between. Star rode up to meet him,

"How is Bear? Is he alive? Where is he? God dammit answer me!"

"Just calm down, my love, it looks like he'll be alright. Only time will tell. He's at the doc's office.

"I'm going to see him," she turned the big gray and was gone.

"Love you," Luke said to no one in particular.

"Is that all?" Luke asked the deputies.

"Yeah these three were in the bunkhouse and didn't want any more. Heard one or two screamin' in the main house, but they didn't come out. As close as we can tell we got 'um all. Raymond George glared at Luke.

"You got something to say, Mr. George? You better think real hard before you speak, 'cause I'm in a real bad mood and I'm lookin' for a reason to blow you off that horse. So please, let's hear it."

Raymond George hung his head and didn't look at Luke the rest of the ride back to town. The sheriff and Star greeted the law officers as they tied off at the hitching post.

"You boys did a real fine job today; real professional and I want to thank you, Luke commended. "Get these men put to bed then join the sheriff and me over at the saloon, I'm buyin."

He walked over to Star and kissed her forehead and said, "I'll see you back at camp after while. I'm gonna spend a little time with the doc. Maybe I can lend a hand."

"Okay, I'll see you in a couple of hours…and I love you too."

"…She did hear," Luke pondered. "Why you little…never mind."

The next day Luke set out to find John Marsh, the brother of the mountain man he killed a year and half or so back. He started at the sheriff's office. Sheriff Gaylord Rose said the name sounded familiar but didn't know where to find him.

"Check with the manager over at the bank. He knows everyone in the valley for one reason or another, and don't take any crap off him."

"I never do," Luke smiled and headed out the door.

First stop: the Doc's. As he walked in, he saw the doc with a very strange look on his face. "Doc…?"

"You ain't gonna believe this; I know I damn well don't! This monster of yers is damn near healed-up. Come look at this!"

They walked to the back room and found Bear sitting on the operating table, his tail wagging and his tongue dripping.

"Look at this, Marshal. These wounds are closed up, or I'm seein' things!"

Luke looked at the bullet holes. They were scabbed over and looked to be several weeks old.

"Grandma, are you messing with me?" he thought.

He gave Bear a hug and rubbed his head. "I'll be back this afternoon."

"Are you talkin' to me or yer dog? the doc asked.

Luke just smiled and shouted back, "Yes!"

He found the skinny, beetle-nosed banker sitting in his office, and Luke walked in without being announced.

"Who the hell are you and what're you doin' in my office? I don't see anyone without an appointment."

Luke put his hands on the banker's desk, looked him in the eye and said, "You'll see me, if you've got any sense at all."

The banker sat up straight in his swivel chair and said, "What is it I can do for you, Marshal?"

"I'm looking for John Marsh."

"May I ask what yer business with Mr Marsh is?

Luke replied, "You can ask, but you won't like the answer."

The banker tried very hard to keep his nerves under control, and Luke could tell he had his attention.

"Across the street, around the corner, turn right on First Street, second office on yer left."

Luke left the bank without a good-bye, kiss my rear, or anything, and the banker didn't take a breath till he saw Luke turn the corner.

Luke saw the sign, "Mash Properties—Ranches and Farms—bought and sold. John Marsh proprietor."

Luke walked straight into the office and looked at the only person in the small room.

"Are you John Marsh?"

He had tucked his badge inside his buckskin shirt.

"Yes Sir, I sure am. How can I be of service today?"

"Bullwhip Mullins sent me to collect two thousand dollars."

"Who the hell are you anyway?" John asked.

Luke was playing with him, "I'm the man that's gonna take Bullwhip his money. He's paying me $200 to get it for him, but truth be told, I woulda got it for twenty and killed ya in the process."

Marsh looked at the 6'4" frame of the man standing in front of him and moved to a large safe and begun to spin the wheel to access the combination.

Luke pushed him a little further, "I hope, for your sake, you're not going to do anything stupid when you open that door, like reach for a gun…'cause it will be the very last thing you ever do."

Luke took a step to his right so he could see the man's hands and most of the inside of the safe—stacks of cash in very neat rows. Marsh counted several bills from one pile and it didn't even reduce the size as far as he could tell. Marsh closed the safe door and sat back down at his desk. He counted out $2000 in fifties and hundreds, and Luke could tell it was killing him to part with the cash. He took the bills and put them in his pouch and decided to mess with Marsh a little more.

"My name is US Marshal Luke Kash, and I'm the man you sent Bullwhip to kill. Didn't quite work out that way. The next time you put a bounty on someone, you'd better make sure the hunter is better than the hunted. In fact, I don't really recommend you hiring any more killers; you're not very good at it." Luke smiled and turned to walk out of the small office, then he stopped and said to Marsh, "You're very lucky that I didn't have time to come for you after I killed Bull, 'cause I surely would have killed you as well. It's been a while, and I have calmed down, but I wouldn't recommend you crossing my path in the future. Do you understand?"

"Yes, Sir, Mr. Kash…I mean, Marshal, I truly do understand."

"I don't ever want to see you again, and I mean that for sure."

"I hope you enjoy yer cash and your trip back, wherever yer headed."

Luke smiled to himself and figured he had given John Marsh enough to think about as he walked back to the bank.

The banker saw Luke coming and said out loud "Oh Lord, not again!" He greeted him and asked, "What else can I do for you, Marshal?"

Luke laid the bills on the banker's desk. "I'd like to change this to gold."

"May I ask why, Marshal?"

"Well, they're not going to stop printing gold and it won't ever be recalled by the government."

The banker thought about it and decided to make some changes in his own investments as well.

Luke rode out to their camp and loaded the wagons for the trail, then he hitched the mules and he and Star headed for town. They had a nice meal at the diner and the sheriff came over and joined them.

"What should I do with all the gear we collected from the George gang?"

Luke thought about it, "Well, it looked to me like there were some pretty good horses and rigs from the ranch, and yer deputies were riding some worn-out mounts. Why don't you fix them up with some good gear and some decent weapons, sell the rest off and make some improvements to your jail."

The sheriff smiled at the idea. "I got a wire from Marshal Simms. He was amazed that the problem is already solved. He said you should take some time off, and he would see you back home when you get there."

Luke pulled the wagons up in front of the Doc's office and went in to collect Bear. He was standing in the front of the office, ready to go.

"What do ya think, Doc?"

"Don't ask me,this is the gall damnedest thing I ever seen, and I ain't kiddin'."

Luke tossed a $50 double-eagle about eight feet in the air, and the doc almost choked when he recognized what it was. He used two hands to catch it to make sure it wouldn't get away.

"I can't make change for this!" he said.

"Don't need any," Luke smiled.

"If you ever get back this way, young fella, it would be my honor to buy ya a drink or three."

"I'll certainly keep that in mind." Luke opened the back door to the wagon and Bear climbed inside as if nothing had ever happened.

"Are you sure he can travel?" Star inquired.

Luke replied, "Take a look," as Bear jumped up on the wagon seat between them.

"How is this even possible? she asked. Luke shrugged and just mumbled, "Grandma, Grandma."

He snapped the reins above the backs of Thunder and Lightning, and they were off. It wasn't long before the mules found their own gait, and they headed southwest toward the indian nation.

Two and a half days later they were sitting around the fire and Star was telling stories of their trip to Denver and back. When she told of how Bear had been shot and his miraculous recovery, Dark Moon just smiled. Luke saw the twinkle in Star's eyes and he knew things would never be the same.

The next morning before sunup, Yellow Eagle was outside the wagon, ready to round up wild horses. Luke had ropes and hobbles and food in his pouch. His Winchester slung over his shoulder, they rode off to the west, Bear running by their sides with no sign that he was ever injured. That evening they were back with six beautiful, young Appaloosas. Luke gave Yellow Eagle his pick—two of the six, and he kept four to sell in Taos.

Luke woke before sunup every morning and spent several hours working with the wild horses, with Bear's help, of course. On the fourth morning, Luke had the wagons packed to travel, and the gray and the new horses tied to the ox-cart. They ate and said their good-byes and were on the trail by the time the sun was breaking the top of the mountain. Storm and Bear moved easily alongside of

Luke's lodge-on-wheels. Bear's wounds were completely healed and his hair had grown back.

About three hours outside of Taos Luke saw a herd of elk grazing on the side of the mountain. He pulled the team up and loaded his Sharps rifle, adjusted the sights for three hundred twenty-five yards and aimed about three feet above the big bull's back allowing for the drop of the bullet as it traveled up-hill. He squeezed the trigger slowly and the big gun bucked. The animal lifted his head to see what all the noise was about. Luke counted to three slowly, and watched the very large elk drop to the ground. Luke untied the gray, took a braided leather rope and jumped on Storm. He called to Bear and they all headed up the mountain to gather the trophy.

That evening, Gunther, his wife and son, Miguel and his wife, and Teddy and Becky all gathered at the ranch and ate elk steak grilled outside over an open fire. Fresh asparagus, flour tortillas and some nuts and berries rounded out the menu, and Becky brought her wonderful berry stuffed buns for dessert. Harvy had delivered five cases of French brandy while they were away, and it didn't take Luke long to pop the cork on one and fill every one's glass. They all laughed and ate and had a grand ol' time. The ranch hands and the cook and her helper ate after the guests were served. Teddy took almost a hundred and fifty pounds of meat back to the butcher shop at the end of the evening and hung it in the smoker. Marshal Simms asked Luke to join him for breakfast the next morning, and he assured him he'd be there. Star and Luke did their part to help the cook and her assistant clean before they wandered off to bed. Luke slid under the covers, just about to close his eyes when Star let her buckskin dress fall to the floor. His eyelids stuck open …and you know the rest.

CHAPTER 10

The next morning just after sunup, Luke walked out on the porch and Star followed. She stood behind him with her arms around his waist and whispered in his ear,

"I love my home, I love my life and I love you, Mr. Kash."

Luke replied, "I love you more," and he stepped onto the hitching post and on to Storm's back. Bear bounded and barked, and they headed down the mountain towards town. Brady Simms was sitting at a table in the cafe when Luke rode up. There was a new gal working that Luke hadn't seen before. He ordered biscuits with gravy and coffee.

"What's on your mind, Brady?"

"I didn't want to ruin the party last night, but the there was some trouble yesterday. Some saddle tramps stopped by the McCracken's ranch and shot them both, then they raped that purdy little daughter of theirs and cut her throat.

We discovered the family about noon, but it looked like it happened in the middle of the night. They ran off their stock, killed that nice dog of theirs and set the place on fire. I'd be on their trail, but I got word that I was needed over round Wagon Mound just before we found them. I'm headed out as soon as we're finished here."

"I'll head back to the ranch and tell Star, then I'll be on my way.

"I'll have her keep an eye on things while we're gone. She's turning into a pretty good hand and one heck of a lawman. Which way do you think they're headed, Brady?" Luke asked.

"The tracks headed south and it looked like they had about six to eight horses and a dozen or so cattle, shouldn't be to hard to follow."

"I'm sure Bear has already got the scent. He barked in confirmation. Luke ordered six eggs, two big slices of ham and four biscuits for Bear, and he ate while the two lawmen finished their coffee and conversation.

"I'll stop by the ranch and see if I can glean any more information before I hit the trail."

"Good thinkin', son. Have I told you how much I appreciate your help?"

"Only every time we see each other. By the way, I brought you a bottle of that French brandy; you seemed to enjoy it and the nights are getting a little nippy. He reached into his pouch and set it on the table. They definitely had a mutual admiration for one another.

Luke rode up to the burned out McCracken ranch house and he could smell death in the air. Storm spooked a little, but then Bear barked and he settled down. Luke jumped down and started to look around the area to see if he could find anything that would help. Some spent 44.40 casings from a Winchester and some 45s. He noticed some tracks from two horses, one with the front left shoe dragging that looked like it might be cracked or even broken, and one without shoes, probably an indian pony, a renegade.

"We'll soon know," he said to Bear. "You ready boy?"

Bear grunted and took off south toward Santa Fe and Storm fell right in behind...fast! Luke saw the killers trail like it had been painted down the middle of the wagon tracks with a brush and white wash. Bear found something as well. He barked and increased his speed and Storm stayed right beside him. They ran what Luke thought was full out, and then he remembered the first time he had ever let Storm go. He was chasing his cousin back to the Ute village and realized that Storm still had at least one more gait left in him, maybe two.

Two hours, three hours, how long could these amazing animals keep up this pace? Neither one showed any sign of tiring or slowing down. Luke finally reined Storm in toward the river, more to relieve himself than for his animals. They drank sparingly and Storm ate a few mouthfuls of fresh green grass. The animals were ready to go as soon as Luke returned from the pee tree.

Luke was up and they were off once again. The trail was getting clearer as they made great time. Luke knew the rustlers weren't moving more than ten maybe twelve miles a day, and he could tell by the signs that the two riders weren't cowboys. Their tracks were all over the place trying to keep the stock together

They rode for another thirty minutes or so, and Luke saw dust up ahead. A few minutes later a wagon came into view. He noticed pots and pans hanging from the side boards and bright red words on the wagon cover, "Rooney's Traveling Show and Medicines."

Luke pulled Storm up beside the wagon and Bear continued on for a hundred yards or so.

"Hey Mister, how you doin'?"

"I'm US Marshal Kash. Have you seen a couple of hombres herding a few horses and some cattle? One may be an indian."

"As a matter a fact, I just past them about three miles back. But there's three of them, not two."

"What's the third one look like?"

"There's a gun fighter, an indian and a half-breed. None of them er cowboys, that's fer sure."

"The third one must have joined them just before you past them, because there's only two riders from here all the way back to Taos."

"What's up, Marshal?"

"Well, Mr. Rooney, they shot a rancher and his wife, and raped their fourteen-year-old daughter. They cut her throat then they burned the place down and shot the stock except for the ones they have with them."

"You won't have any problem catching them; they don't have a damn bit of control over those animals."

"Thanks, Mr Rooney, I hope they've had fun 'cause it's coming to an end very rapidly."

Luke turned Storm and kicked him in the flanks, and three strides later he was running at full-speed. They caught up with Bear and he fell in cadence with the big horse.

About ten minutes later Luke saw the trail dust, but only two riders. He slowed Storm to get a better look and a bullet creased his left arm. He pulled Storm to the left and pointed to the right for Bear and he sprinted away into the brush and mesquite bushes. Luke noticed the neither one of the riders was an indian. He must be the bushwhacker. He pulled his Sharps 52-caliber and grabbed a couple of rounds from his pouch, opened the breech and slid a bullet into the chamber. He waited until he heard the blood-chilling scream from across the trail, then he took aim and blew the top of the head off the nearest rider to him. He broke open the long gun and loaded the second round just as the brass from the first shot ejected, snapped the receiver closed and took careful aim. The third rider was on a solid black horse and it looked pretty fast, but Luke would bet a lot of gold that it couldn't outrun a 52-caliber slug. This last rider was bent over low in the saddle to present a smaller target for Luke. No matter, he was only about two hundred yards away. Luke let him run. The outlaw was sure no one could hit him from this distance now, about three hundred fifty yards, maybe more. Luke stood beside Storm and rested his rifle on the big horse's back, pulled it in tight to his shoulder, sighted down the barrel and squeezed the trigger gently. The big gun jumped. He almost lost it when he fired, forgetting about the wound in his left bicep.

"Oh yeah! That hurts!" he winced.

He was waiting for Bear when Rooney rode up on one of his work horses and they were both breathing heavily.

"Son of a bitch, boy. That was some kinda shootin'. Where's the big ol' dog of yer's?"

Luke pointed across the trail and Bear was coming in their direction carrying something in his mouth. He ran up to Luke and dropped the last two fingers of a left hand at his feet.

"God damn," said Rooney. "That's purdy impressive. Where's the rest of him?" he asked.

"Over on the other side of the trail, but if you have a queasy stomach I wouldn't go over there. What are you doing here, Mr. Rooney?"

"Well, thought ya might need a hand, then I realized who you were and I slowed ol' Smokey down so he wouldn't die on me."

"Why would you want to get in the middle of a gun fight?"

"Just outta habit, I guess. I do have a little experience, ya know."

"What do you mean, Mr Rooney?"

"Damn it, quit callin' me mister. It used to be marshal, but now it's just plain Rooney."

"Marshal?" Luke asked. "What happened?"

"I guess I just got tired of shootin' folks and havin' them shoot me."

"I didn't know you could walk away from the marshal's service," Luke wondered.

"Well, most of the time ya get carried away in a pine box, but if ya make it past twenty years, they give ya a few bucks a month. It's not enough to have a decent roof over yer head, but you can get by if you can find somethin' else to do."

About that time, Luke saw Rooney's wagon coming down the trail.

"That's my best friend Ersla. She dances, sings like a bird and she's damn good at sellin' a bottle of snake oil. Oh yeah, and she purdy good at patchin' up gunshot holes, too."

Ersla stepped down from the wagon and shook hands with Luke.

"Rooney, dammit! I told ya he wouldn't need any help."

"Just patch him up. I'm gonna walk across the trail fer a minute."

A few minutes later, Rooney came walking back with a holster and six-gun slung over his shoulder and a good-looking repeating rifle in his hand.

"What a goddamn mess yer big ol' dog makes."

"Yeah, you're much better off staying on his good side. Where are you heading? Luke asked.

"On our way to Taos if these ol' nags don't break down on us."

Luke looked down the trail and said, "There's a couple of pretty well-trained horses over there, and the owner won't be coming for them."

Rooney and Luke rounded up the stock and Luke picked out the best two horses to pull the medicine show wagon. Rooney asked Luke if he could use some company into Taos.

"Sure, why not. My boys need a little easy traveling." He was getting a good feeling about the grizzly ol' gunslinger and his lady.

Bear headed the the small herd north and kept them on the trail. He made it look easy. They loaded the killers' saddles and guns, and turned their horses loose knowing they'd probably follow the rest of the stock back to Taos; and they were right. Luke and Bear moved the stock into the corral at the McCracken ranch. He would send someone from town out in the morning to make sure they had feed and water. He and Bear caught up with Rooney and rode beside the wagon and the three made small talk.

"What are your plans?" Luke asked him.

"Find a place to camp and rest up for a few days, then head on east."

"I have the perfect spot to park your wagon and rest your bones a while."

"Well, thank you very much, Marshal. Lead on, my young friend."

They crossed the stream behind the butcher shop about 3:30 in the after noon, and Teddy and Becky came out and waved. Luke turned Storm around and rode back to Teddy.

"I have some business to discuss with you and and I'll be back later on or first thing in the morning."

He smiled and headed up the hill to catch up with Rooney. Luke guided Rooney to a beautiful spot under a grove of oaks and pines by a running stream, about thirty yards from the ranch house. There was a crystal clear pool that Luke had made by damming up some large rocks. He and Star used it for bathing when the weather allowed. Star walked down from the main house and hugged and kissed Luke. She saw the bloody hole in the arm of his buckskins and asked, "Are you alright?"

"Yep!" Ersla and Grandma took care of it.

She met Rooney and Ersla. They had a natural smile and Star felt warmth from the couple.

"Dinner will be ready in about an hour," she announced, and headed back to the ranch to oversee the evening meal.

CHAPTER 11

They dined on green chili stew, fired pinto beans and fresh vegetables that Luke hadn't had before. They looked like potatoes but had a stronger taste. Although the cook had them covered in fresh butter and some kind of green garnish, Luke wasn't exactly sure about them. Star told him the Mexican cook called them "el nabo." Proud that she was becoming very proficient in Spanish, she declared, "That means turnips."

Luke replied, "I can do very well without them in the future. In fact…you might see if the horses like them." Everyone laughed.

"Well, I like them," she replied, "and if you don't eat your vegetables, you won't get any of Rosita's special dessert."

Luke rolled a couple of chunks around in the stew then put them in a tortilla and forced them down. He pushed his plate away and tried to smile.

"You did good, my love," Luke affirmed, and she cleared the plates and went into the kitchen. Star soon returned with a large platter of sopaipillas, a fried pastry, and Luke was back in heaven. Rosita served fresh local honey and sugar mixed with cinnamon with her creation.

"Oh my goodness! Rosita, these smell wonderful!"

"Thank you, Meester Luke, I hope you in-joy."

Luke broke out glasses and a bottle of the French brandy, and they laughed and ate and drank, and enjoyed the rest of the evening. Luke snuck off to the kitchen and put his arm around Rosita's shoulders. He told her what a wonderful job she had done and dropped a gold coin in her apron pocket. Rosita came back with a pot of hot coffee and served it in their porcelain mugs …and life was good.

Rooney asked, "Do you always eat like this?"

Luke smiled, "When were at home we try to. Although Star's a pretty darn good trail cook."

Luke showed the couple to the extra bedroom under the stairs and said good-night.

Star watched Luke as he undressed and saw the blood-covered bandage. She came to him and unwrapped it. Not surprisingly, the wound was nearly healed.

"Your grandma is certainly keeping a close watch on you." Luke smiled and nodded.

The next morning, Luke and Rooney sat on the porch with a cup of Rosita's coffee and watched the town below come alive. Rooney had one of the killers' six-guns strapped on and tied down low on the right side, like a gun fighter.

"I'll pay you fer this as soon as I make a money transfer at the bank. Had to sell mine for some travelin' money."

"Don't worry about it. A man needs a good pistol. It's yours. I have to go into town and take care of some business. You're welcome to tag along?"

"Sure. I need to pick up some supplies. I'll hitch the horses and be with you in a bit, Luke.

"Don't bother. I have some pretty good saddle horses. I'll have one brought up. I'll have someone come get the tack and weapons out of your wagon in a while, too.

They rode up to the back fence of Gunther's livery and Luke met him about half way. He introduced Rooney and then took him to meet Miguel. Luke left him in Miguel's good care while he went out to take care of business with his partner. Luke told Gunther about the horses and cattle at the ranch.

"I made sure they had feed and water yesterday. You can bring the horses into town to sell, and I'll take care of the details with the bank. I'll have Teddy take care of the cattle and rest of the stock." Then Luke remembered, "Oh yeah, there's also some guns and saddles up at the ranch in Rooney's wagon."

"I'll get it all picked up," Gunther said, and they shook hands.

Luke and Rooney rode around the livery and out onto Main Street, heading north. Luke saw old Hank with his wheel-barrow and shovel coming down the other side of the street picking up the horse droppings from the afternoon and night before. He rode over and greeted him, flipped him a gold coin and kept on going. He pointed to the diner and told Rooney to go get some Joe. He said he'd be back shortly and they'd have breakfast.

Luke stepped up on the boardwalk in front of the bank and banged on the heavy door. He knew that Mr. Weathers, the manager, was in there. He was never far from his money. Weathers peeked through the heavy green canvas curtain, saw Luke and his heart dropped.

"Oh lord, what now?" he thought. "Just a minute, Marshal. Let me get the key. I'll be right with you."

Luke sat in the manager's office, "You heard about the McCrackens?"

"Yes Sir. What a shame. That beautiful little girl…She and my son were very close friends…just terrible."

"Can you tell me how much they owed on their ranch?"

Weathers looked at Luke and thought, "Shit! Here we go again." He pulled his ledger from a drawer and opened it to a marked page. Luke could tell he had already been viewing the account and probably knew the answers that Luke was seeking without looking. He pretended to search the page.

"Yes Sir….Here we go….They owed a balance of $4,328, but they were a month behind, so there were some penalty charges.

"How about the livestock?" Luke asked.

"No Sir, I don't have anything owing on the animals."

"Okay. Take the money from one of my accounts, including your penalty, of course, and pay the property of. I'll come by after lunch and sign the papers and get the title. Make the title out to Mr and Mrs Moore, my partners, and show it free and clear of any liens."

"But...Umm...But...."

"Yes?" Luke stopped in mid-stride and turned to look at the banker, "Was there something else?

The banker thought better of saying what was on his mind, and replied, "No Sir, Everything will be ready right after noon, Sir."

"Thank you. I'll see you then," and Luke walked out.

Luke and Rooney ate ham steaks, four fried eggs, a big plate of biscuits and gravy and a pot of hot coffee. Bear did the same, minus the coffee. Luke left his usual gold coin on the table and they headed across the street to meet with Teddy.

Rooney said to Luke, "I've noticed, you throw money around like it was...I don't know what."

"Ya know, Rooney, I've been very lucky in the last few years, and if I can't help my friends then my money is just like a pocket full of rocks. It just seems to keep coming my way, and that's fine. But I have way more than I'll ever need, so I share. It makes me feel good."

Luke made the introductions and they sat and had one more cup of joe. Becky did make great coffee.He told Teddy about the cattle and what ever else he could gather at the McCracken ranch, and that they owned the whole thing now. Teddy just shook his head and everyone smiled. Luke said he had plans to rebuild the ranch house and that they should meet him out there about three o'clock. Teddy and Becky stared at Luke, not quite grasping what he had said or meant.

"Why do you need us?" Becky asked.

"Well," Luke answered, "the town is growing and we need to expand the shop and you're going to need a new place to live. Wouldn't you like to be involved in designing your new home, Becky?

She started to cry. "Really? A home of our own?"

Nothing's too good for my partners. You've done a great job and you deserve it. I'll see you there." And he walked out the door. Rooney just smiled and shook his head and followed.

Luke and Rooney rode up the street to the marshal's office. Luke unlocked the door and removed a note that was nailed to it, and went inside. It was a wire from Captain Simms, US marshal's office,

"Looks like Brady got himself a promotion."

"Is that Marshal Brady Simms? Rooney asked.

"Sure is. The finest man I know,"

"Yeah, I know. We been friends for over twenty years," Rooney reminisced. "I lost track of him 'bout five years back. Where is he?"

"About 60 miles from here mopping up a problem. Says he's heading back tomorrow."

"I can't wait to see him," Rooney smiled at the thought of reuniting with his old friend.

Luke went through a couple of new wanted posters and memorized the faces and names; then walked next door to the telegraph office and sent a return wire to Captain Simms. Soon, he made his way back to the bank where Weathers had his paperwork ready. Luke read through it, then signed the papers and got a bill of sale and the clear title to the hundred-acre ranch. He put the paperwork in his pouch.

"My friend here, Deputy Marshal Rooney, needs your help. If there's any problem, give him what he needs and take it from my account until you get it straightened out."

"Yes Sir, Marshal, not a problem at all, Sir.

CHAPTER 12

Luke left Rooney at the bank and went over to the Welcome Inn to pay Harvy for the brandy and to have a cold beer. He'd been going non-stop since before sunup. He walked in and looked around. The seven other fellows in the bar were all known to Luke, so he went to the bar and shook hands with Harvy.

"How are you, my friend?"

"Doin' well, Marshal. Life ain't too bad, all things considered. Got some ice cold beer if ya want one."

"Sounds good to me."

Luke acknowledged everyone in the bar from his corner spot where he could see the whole room. Harvy came back with a large schooner of very cold beer. Luke took a long pull and closed his eyes.

"Ambrosia," he thought to himself.

He threw a $5 gold piece, and asked Harvy to get everyone a drink. Luke turned back toward the bar and heard two rapid gunshots. Then a shotgun blast took out the twenty-foot mirror behind bar. He put his hand on the grip of his holstered over and under as he turned to see the swinging doors fly open and a man fall backward through them. The man turned and fell face-down on the planked floor; his shotgun sliding from his hand, rattling around and coming to rest on the bar floor. Rooney stepped up on the boardwalk and looked over the swinging doors.

"Got beer?"

"Damn, Rooney. You're a troublemaker. Can't you see I'm trying to have a quiet glass of beer with my friend Harvy here?"

"Do you know this guy?" Rooney asked, motioning to the man on the floor.

"Never seen him before," Luke answered.

Harvy piped up. "He's been hangin' around since yesterday afternoon stayin' to himself, not saying much; but he obviously knew you, Marshal....I was just thinkin about a new mirror—a little longer, a little bigger."

Luke walked over and went through the dead man's pockets, and found sixty-three dollars, a couple of horseshoe nails, some silver coins and four 12-gauge shotgun shells. He unbuckled his gun belt and a folded piece of paper fell to the floor. Luke unfolded the hand-written note and it read, "$500 Bring me the head of Luke Kash, Taos, N.M.." It was signed, J. Marsh, Denver, Colorado.

"Son of a bitch! Some folks are just too stupid for their own good. This idiot is dead and doesn't even know it," Luke said in a low tone.

"Do you know him now?" Rooney asked.

"No, but I know the dead man on the other end of this note."

Luke turned to Harvy, "I guess you'd better order that mirror. Send me the bill if this doesn't cover it," and he threw the dead man's money on the bar.

"Did you see his horse?" Luke questioned Rooney.

"Nah….He musta stashed it."

At that very moment, Gunther walked into the saloon, asking, "Everyone alright in here?" as he stepped over the corpse on the floor.

"Yes, we're fine, but Harvy's mirror is dead," Rooney chuckled.

"Do you have this hombre's rig?" Luke asked.

"Got both of 'em:" Gunther replied, "a really nice black, 'bout three years old; a fine pack-mule; couple of rifles, a long one and a Winchester; and a good supply of ammo…two hundred and fifty in gold too!"

"Sounds like he got a deposit up front," Luke pondered. "Sort his stuff out and see what it's worth, and I'll check with you before I leave for Denver."

"Denver? I didn't know you were goin' back to Denver," Gunther sounded surprised.

"I didn't either, until a few minutes ago…but I am. Crap! It's time for me to meet Becky and Teddy. You comin' Rooney?"

"No, I think I'll stick around here for a while".

"I'll stop back by on my way home to see if you're still here."

"No problem. Barkeep, how 'bout some beer for me and my friends?" Rooney bellied up to the bar as he reloaded his hand gun.

Luke and the carpenter that was in charge of building his home rode south. They saw Teddy's and Becky's wagons not far ahead. They all arrived at the McCracken's ranch within minutes of each other. He showed the builder around and had Becky tell him what she really wanted for her home. Every time she would draw a room in the sand, Luke would look at the size and double it. By the time he was finished, it was around 1,800 square feet and Becky couldn't believe what was happening. Four bedrooms, a kitchen, dining room: a dream home!

"How long are we talking about?" Luke asked.

"'Bout three months, I guess."

"How about 3 weeks?"

"Three weeks? It'll take twenty men to get it done in three weeks."

"Get it done."

"Yes Sir, Marshal."

"Becky you ever built a house before?" Luke asked.

"No Sir, never!"

"Well, you'd better get ready 'cause you're in charge; and if it's not the way you want it, we'll tear it down and start over, understand?"

Luke opened his pouch and handed Becky the paid title to the property.

"Here, this is for you…for ever and ever, your home."

She hugged his neck and tried to kiss his forehead but she couldn't reach, so she settled for his neck. Luke blushed and said, "I gotta go. Headed for Denver."

He jumped up on Storm and kicked him in the flanks and they were off like the wind.

"Rooney, would you keep an eye on things while I'm gone?"

"I'd really like to, but I won't able."

"Why's that?"

"'Cause I'm goin' to Denver!"

"You'll need a better horse if you're going with me. You can take Star's gray. She's the only horse in three states that can come close to staying with Storm."

"Is he really that fast?"

"…And then some."

They left town at 4:30, about twenty minutes before sundown.

"Don't cha think we should wait 'til morning, Luke?"

"Do whatever you like," and Luke turned Storm and nudged him in the girth with his heels, and the big horse took off with Bear by their side, Rooney bringing up the rear and riding hard to catch up.

Luke ran them hard 'til after midnight, then he pulled up at one of the camping spots along the river just before the turn off to the Ute Village. He wasn't going to turn; he was following the river all the way to Denver and Lord help any one that got in his way. About three hours before sunup, Luke threw a rock and hit Rooney in the knee. He came up with his shooter in his hand pointed straight at Luke's head. He holstered it and saddled the gray. Luke was already on the trail and he had to hustle not to get left behind again.

At 4:00 that afternoon, Luke could see the rooftops of Denver. He hadn't said a word since they left Taos, and Rooney was wondering what the hell was going on.

"Is that Denver? It can't be. It's four hard days from Taos."

"Apparently not," Luke replied. "I'll meet you at the saloon across from the sheriff's office. He nudged Storm and he jumped forward and hit a pace that Rooney had never seen from an animal in his life. They were out of sight in about forty-five seconds and the gray was doing a good job of running, but no threat to Storm.

CHAPTER 13

L uke dropped the lead rope from the hackamore on the ground just outside of J. Marsh's office. He stepped up on the boardwalk, and in one fluid motion kicked the door off its hinges and continued into the small room. Marsh didn't have time to focus his eyes.

"What the hell!?" Then he saw Luke. His blood ran ice cold.

"You have to be the dumbest son of a bitch on earth! Are you deaf?"

"N…n…no Sir!"

"Did you not understand me the last time I was here?"

"Y…yes Sir!"

"Did you think I was kidding?"

"N...no sir!"

"Then what the hell happened?"

"Yaaaou happened! You killed my brother!"

Luke was fuming, "Yes! Yes, I did, and now I'm gonna kill you. Open the safe and don't even breathe or I'll blow your head all over your office."

Marsh wet himself while he was opening the safe, and Luke didn't feel a bit sorry for him

"Put the money on your desk, and if you're about half-smart, which I'm beginning to doubt, you may live for a little while longer."

Luke took several stacks of fifties and hundreds and filled his pouch.

"Now put the rest back." Marsh looked puzzled and surprised. He started to put the balance of the cash back in the safe. Maybe he would live through the night after all.

"Why aren't you taking all the money?" he tried to engage Luke in conversation, but he wasn't playing. He had been warned and Luke didn't give two warnings.

"I'm not a thief. You're just compensating me for my very valuable time. Do you have a horse?"

"Yes, out back, but he's not saddled."

"No matter. We're not going that far." Luke helped him up on his worn-out old plow horse. He whistled for Storm and he came running around the building with Bear at his heels.

"Bring him, Bear, and the dog took the reins of the tired old horse in his mouth and led it off behind Storm into the forest. They rode for about thirty minutes up the canyon north of town. Luke found what he was looking for and reined in Storm. Bear followed.

"Get down and sit on that rock over there."

The skinny business man complied. Luke walked up to within a foot or so of his face and bent down.

Luke looked him in the eye and said, "You really don't understand do you, Marsh?"

For some reason, he had regained some of his courage, "Yer not gonna kill me. Yer a US Marshal!"

Luke pulled his Colt PeaceMaker and shot him between the eyes.

"You really were a stupid bastard," he said, to no one in particular.

He turned the plow horse loose to go home to the feed bag while he dragged Marsh behind a couple of large boulders where no one but the wolves would find him; then he rode off to the South.

Before he had gone a mile, he heard a wolf howl. Then he heard two more answering. …His work was done.

He skirted the town and then rode back up the road to meet Rooney. He was ready for a beer, some food and some serious sleep. The barkeep recognized Luke immediately and brought him a beer.

"How ya doin' Marshal? Back so soon?"

"Just passing through. Have you got a couple of quiet rooms?"

"No, but I got one with two beds in it. And if any one disturbs ya, K.C. over there will put a load of buckshot in their ass."

"Great. How about a couple of beef steaks before we hit the sack?" Luke tossed him a $20 gold piece.

"I'll have K.C. put a couple of buckets of hot water in yer room so you can clean up."

After they ate, Luke flipped K.C. a $5 gold piece as they walked by.

"G'night," Luke said as he and Rooney went up.

The next morning at sunup they had hot biscuits, cream gravy with sausage and coffee at the diner, and Bear came up to meet them. He had spent the night in the livery stable with his best bud. Luke ordered a platter of scrambled eggs and potatoes for his giant friend.

Luke woke up the clerk in the telegraph office and sent two wires: one to Captain Brady Simms and one to Morning Star. Soon they were off, heading south at a much slower pace than on the trip to Denver. Luke was more sociable than he had been for the last thirty-six hours, so Rooney knew it was okay to ask some questions.

"So, my young friend, did we get our business taken care of?"

"Yes, we did. You know, my client was a very arrogant person. I explained the situation to him not two weeks ago and he assured me he understood. Then, the man you dropped at the saloon showed me that he didn't hear a word I said."

"It was a very expensive mistake on his part," Rooney mused.

Luke had found the time to count the cash in his pouch and it turned out to be over $12,000. Luke smiled and guessed there must have been several hundred thousand in Marsh's safe. No one would ever guess there had been a robbery; and his family,if he had one, would be able to get by.

"I have $2000 for you, for your trouble," Luke said to Rooney.

"I didn't have any trouble? What are you talking about?"

"I believe that people need to be paid for their time and that's for you, and that's the end of that."

Rooney knew not to argue with the young marshal; something that several folks had failed to figure out in the past few years. And it got them a one-way trip to Potter's Field.

On the journey home, they talked about everything from marshaling, to ranching, to fast horses and big dogs, to indian tribes and bank robbers; and Rooney decided Marshal Luke Kash was the real deal and would be a very good friend to have. Luke had come to the same conclusion about Rooney.

Captain Brady Simms was at his desk when Luke walked in with Rooney close behind.

"How ya doin' Luke?" he asked without looking up.

"Doing well, Captain."

"You even look like a captain," Rooney offered.

"Oh my god! Is that Rooney, my good friend? Where the hell have you been? I been tryin' to run you down fer nigh on five years now!"

"Well, been roamin' 'round tryin' to stay out of trouble, but I think them days are over. Young Luke here has got me a-hankerin' to get back into action again."

"Have ya lost any steam in the last few years?" Simms asked.

"Not so's I can tell."

"He saved my bacon the other day," Luke added.

"I just happened to be in the right place at the right time."

"Yes, and just happened to be a very good shot as well."

"Ya want a badge?" the captain asked. "The pay's a little better then it was five years ago and I got a house just off Main Street if yer interested?"

"Ah hell, I was hopin' to bunk up at Luke's place. They live a little different up there and I kinda got used to it." Everyone laughed.

"Raise yer right hand. Do you swear…" And just like that, Rooney was a US Marshal once again.

Two weeks later the threesome was sipping some very good whisky at the Welcome Inn. Harvy, the barkeep, was hanging around visiting with the lawmen and admiring his new mirror when three men tied up to the hitching post and clomped into the saloon.

"Barkeep, give us a bottle of the cheap shit and some beers to cut the taste with!"

Harvy moved away from the marshals at the end of the bar and set a bottle of rot-gut and three shot glasses in front of the men. He went to draw their beer and as he turned, one of the saddle tramps threw a shot glass that ricocheted off the side of Harvy's head and landed in the middle of the marshal's drinks, breaking two of the three glasses and knocking their bottle over. Luke grabbed it before it landed on its side, and sat it back up.All three marshals turned and Luke put a hand on each of their shoulders.

"I got this." Luke stepped forward, "Hey fellas. What's the problem? Did Harvy here do something wrong?"

"Who the hell is Harvy?"

"The man you just hit in the head with that glass."

"Well, that was an accident. I was aimin' at you." And the three laughed out loud.

"Are you as bad a shot with your pistol as you are throwing a shot glass?"

"Maybe you'd like to find out."

"Well, if you don't apologize to Harvy and buy us a drink of good whisky, maybe I would."

"We sure as hell ain't buyin' you sons a bitches no whisky!"

"Well, then I guess you got a problem," Luke stated.

"Why? You three green horns gonna brace us?" He chuckled.

"Actually, no….Just me."

And the three strangers laughed out loud.

"You need to go get ready, Squirt?"

"No, I'm as ready as I'm gonna get." Luke assured him.

The other two turned and moved to each side of their cocky partner, and they were trying to keep from laughing out loud.

"I hope you got enough money between you to pay yer bar bill 'cause I'm gonna be really pissed off if I have to cover your tab too. By the way, you got yer momma's address on you so I can let kin know where you're buried?"

They looked shocked. Luke stared them in the eyes and the instant the first one twitched, Luke made his move; so quickly no one was sure they saw it. His hand hit the grip of the 20-gauge over and under, and both barrels exploded. Eight pieces of lead from each barrel tore into the middle man and the one on his left, and knocked them backwards off their feet. Neither one had cleared leather.

His hand moved to the grip of his Colt in his cross-draw holster. He pulled it, cocked the hammer with his thumb and fired; then fanned the hammer one more time with the trigger still held back. It sounded like one single shot, but two separate 45 slugs hit the third man in his forehead about a half inch apart. He staggered back, taking two wobbly steps, and crumbled to the floor, face-down in an ever widening puddle of blood; hand still on his gun, gun still in his holster.

"Holy crap! I ain't never seen nothin' like that," Rooney gasped.

"Where the hell did you learn that?" Brady chimed in.

"Ya don't learn somethin' like that," Rooney declared. "Ya either have it, or ya dream about havin' it. And if yer dreamin' 'bout it, ya never will."

"Some people just don't understand," Luke pondered. "Do ya think I should have shown him my badge?"

"Do you think it would have made a difference?" Brady asked.

Luke looked at Rooney and Rooney just shrugged.

"No," Luke concluded.

"I don't either," replied the captain. "You okay, Harvy?"

"I'm gonna have a knot where I got thumped, but it ain't nothin' a couple of shots of that good whisky won't fix up."

Gunther and Miguel came busting through the swinging doors.

"Is ever one alright?"

While Luke told them about the weapons and rigs outside, Brady and Rooney had another drink.

"Where the hell did ya find him?" Rooney asked.

"He showed up in town about five years ago with that horse and some farm animals, and the ol' folks at the butcher shop took a likin' to him and vice-versa. Now he owns just about everything around. He's got some purdy high connections in the Ute nation; his grandmama is the shaman, or somethin', and I think she keeps a purdy close eye on him."

"Yeah, he caught a slug in his left arm out on the trail the day we met, but by the time we got back to town it was nearly healed."

"That's Grandmama," Brady said.

"…And he gave me two thousand bucks fer ridin' to Denver and back with him."

"Yeah, he's a very generous young man. He has me fixed up purdy good for retirement too, and I live on a real nice piece of land that he gave me. Just the damnedest kid I ever met, that's fer sure."

Luke walked back over and asked Harvy for a beer. He was completely out of the mood for whisky.

Thirty minutes later, the north-bound stage came smoking into town. The driver had a bullet in his left shoulder, the shotgun rider and the passengers were missing.The driver, wincing in pain, tried to tell the marshals what had happened.

"We were ambushed!...Four, maybe five men, couldn't tell fer sure. I saw three but one or two more were shootin from cover. They got my shotgunner and my passengers: two men and two women, 'bout six miles back."

Luke grabbed his long gun that was leaning against the bar and looked at the other two marshals. "I'm on my way."

He jumped up on Storm and touched the big horse's flanks with his heels. They were off, headed south with Bear running at their side. Luke rode hard along the trail thinking of his mother and father. He thought they would be proud of him: his continued education, his business sense, his wife and everything he had accomplished in five short years…except maybe for the men he had killed. Then he remembered something his father and grandmother had both said to him.

"Once you accept who you are, then you can accept what you have done."

Luke had no problem accepting what he had done. As far as he could tell, he was born for this life. He didn't want to kill men, but he had no problem with it when it happened.

Luke saw the corpses lying on the trail about a hundred and fifty yards ahead, and he slowed Storm and Bear so he could check his surroundings. He sent Bear out to the right to circle around and check for bushwhackers, and he moved off the trail to the left to make his way closer to the bodies without being a sitting duck. He approached the bodies from the east and Bear came wandering in from the west. There was no sign of trouble, so Luke relaxed a bit.

All the dead had been scavenged. The men had lost their boots, their jackets and pants. Luke couldn't tell if they had been carrying guns or not, and the women were stripped of their clothes, which were in piles off to the side. Luke didn't want to know if they had been raped or not; he was going to assume that they had and was going to treat the robbers accordingly. He moved the bodies off the trail and covered the ladies with their clothes.

He mounted Storm and called Bear and they were off, this time in full-tracking mode. Luke read the trail, Bear sniffed the trail and Storm ran the trail, and between the three, they moved swiftly. About ten miles south of Taos, the trail turned to the west into the forest and higher in elevation. Luke commented to Bear and Storm, "Their first mistake."

Storm whinnied and Bear grunted, and Luke sent Bear on ahead to see what he could see. Luke continued to follow the tracks into the heavy timber and up the mountain when he saw Bear coming back down working his way between the trees at a very fast pace. Luke pulled Storm to a halt and Bear came up beside them. He turned and pointed up the mountain with his muzzle and growled very low; Luke knew they were close. He jumped down and dropped the lead to the hackamore and told Storm to stay. He checked his Winchester and his Sharps and he headed up the mountain on foot. He signaled for Bear to go to the right and he moved to the left so as not to be seen if someone was tracking him back down, which was very unlikely. Luke moved almost silently through the trees and about a half mile farther on, he came upon the camp of the robbers. He left his long rifle against a tree and crawled with his Winchester across his forearms to within fifty yards of their camp.

He could see a couple of the robbers dancing around the campfire in their new duds and trading off taking pulls on a jug. They seemed to be drunk and Luke decided they wouldn't be the first ones to catch a bullet. He saw three more sitting around the fire with tin plates and forks in their hands not paying any attention to their surroundings. Luke crawled up behind a large boulder and braced his Winchester on it. He squeezed the trigger and the farthest man from him in the camp fell backward with a bullet in his head, his plate of beans landing upside down on his face. Luke levered another round into the breech of the rifle and squeezed the trigger, hitting the next man in the chest. He stumbled back and tripped over the dead man behind him, his plate of beans falling to the ground as he collapsed on top of the first.

Bear reacted to his master's gunshots and he sprung from his spot. He flew through the air over the two dead men hitting the third from behind and knocking him face-down into the fire. He came up screaming and trying to brush the embers and fire out of his eyes, hair and beard. Bear grabbed one of his ankles and dragged him back from the fire, moving forward and grabbing the man's neck in his gigantic mouth and snapping it like a twig.

This all happened so fast, the inebriated pair of dancers weren't even aware of what had just taken place. When one of the dancing hombres realized that there were dead people laying around the camp fire, he took off running down the mountain. It took him three to four steps to realize that he didn't have his boots on, and every foot fall landed on dry branches, rocks or small forest critters. The pain was starting to sober him up rapidly. Just as he was about to try and get back up to camp, Luke put a 44.40 bullet in his heart. His chest stopped, but the forward motion of his feet continued until he was horizontal. He seemed to stop in mid-air then fell to the ground.

Bear had landed hard on the last man in camp, and Luke yelled "Bear hold!"

The giant of a dog had the man face-down in the dirt and the dust was coming out the side of the drunk's mouth as he tried to catch his breath. Luke moved into the camp cautiously with his Winchester at the ready; he had the feeling that there was at least one more. He was pretty sure he wouldn't show his face but would try to ambush Luke. He had just caught the image of a man beside a tree about fifteen yards away when an arrow hit him in the right side of his chest. Luke couldn't believe he let someone take him by surprise. He stood still for a short time and then another arrow hit him in his right thigh and then another in the left side of his abdomen just above his cartridge belt. He went down to the ground on his knees and then fell to his back.

Bear came to his side and he ordered the big dog, "Get help. Bring Star," and Bear headed down the mountain at full-speed, jumping fallen trees and bushes and leaping off boulders, running faster then anyone could imagine. Luke laid on a large sharp rock, but hardly felt it poking a hole in his back. Everything was very strange and he felt like he was floating on a cloud. He could see the arrows sticking out of his body, but he wasn't in a lot of pain; he just couldn't move. He saw the half-breed indian standing over him and heard him say "You were good, Marshal, just not good enough," and he walked away.

Luke was confused. The outlaw obviously thought he was dead, although Luke could clearly see him and would never forget his face. He closed his eyes and tried to focus.

"Grandmother, where are you? I need you!" He heard strange musical notes and tribal drums, and then his grandmother's soft voice.

"I'm here, my son. Just rest and breathe easy," and her voice faded away.

When Luke awoke he was lying on his bed in his lodge, and it was moving at a good pace. Star and Bear were by his side and old Doc Burns was standing over him, trying to keep his balance and still treat him. Star held his hand and Bear licked his face, and Luke faded off to sleep once more.

The doc said to Star, "I don't understand. Three wounds and surgery to remove the arrow heads and there was very little bleeding. A normal man would have bled out before we got back to him."

Star grinned and said, "Doctor Burns, don't you know by now that Luke is far from being a normal man."

Two days later, Luke woke in his own bed with vague memories of the ride back to town.

He moved his right arm…no pain. He moved his right leg…no pain. He touched his stomach and there was no bandage and no pain. "Thank you, Grandmother," he thought.

He dressed in brown denim pants, a buckskin shirt and moccasins, and buckled on his gun belt. He checked his over and under in his holster and then the Colt PeaceMaker in his cross-draw holster on his left hip, then he made his way down stairs.

Star and Rosita, the cook, were in the kitchen, and they both beamed when they saw him. Coffee and some eggs and ham, some squaw bread with honey and he felt good as new. He said softly, "Thank you, Grandmother."

He and Morning Star talked for a while as they rocked in the fresh crisp air on their porch and enjoyed another cup of coffee, Bear at their feet.

"I need to go find a halfbreed," he informed her.

"I'm coming with you; I'm starting to get wigwam fever," and they both smiled.

"Let me go check in with Brady then I'll come back and hook up the wagons."

Luke walked in on the captain as he was going through some new wanted posters. He looked at the young marshal and asked, "You healed?"

"Pretty much, I guess. You know about my grandma, right?"

"Yeah. I don't understand it, but I know. Here,take a look at these and put 'em in yer head."

When Luke finished memorizing the new posters he went to the drawer where the others were kept and began to thumb through the stack. He had perused through fifteen or so when the face of the halfbreed that shot him jumped off the page. He took the poster and handed it to Brady. "There ya go."

He told Luke that Rooney was on the trail of the shooter from the ambush, and they were headed north through the mountains toward indian territory.

"The last telegram I got from him was earlier this morning from Tres Piedras."

"Star and I are heading that direction. I need to sit down with my grandparents before winter sets in. Oh, the next time you send Rooney a wire, tell him I'm on my way and don't get himself hurt 'til I get there."

"Will do, and travel safe, my friend," Brady said as the two shook hands.

Two hours later Luke, Morning Star and their herd were on the trail about a half mile north of Taos, and he was feeling 100%.

"Nothing like fresh air to bring you back to good health; there must be more than half an indian in me," he thought as he breathed deeply.

About three in afternoon they were in Tres Piedras and Luke pulled the wagons up to the sheriff's office. He jumped down and went in. The sheriff informed him that Rooney was headed back into the forest going northwest. Luke told Star to keep going toward their village and keep the shotgun by her side at all times. He told Bear to stay with her, and he barked that he understood.

Luke had his Winchester on a strap over his shoulder along with his pouch of supplies and his long gun across his thighs as he rode. He saw Rooney's trail very clearly, he was purposely riding close to bushes to break branches and knock off leaves, and Luke could see it fifty yards ahead. It was only a few hours old. He put Storm into a fast gallop and it was as if the big horse could see the trail as clearly as his rider.

From the distance between the roans' hoof prints, Luke could tell they were traveling much faster than Rooney, and they would be catching up with him before long. Luke and Storm had been in deep forest for less than an hour and Rooney's trail was blazing hot. He rode about a quarter of a mile and Luke saw the roan grazing in some deep grass…no sign of Rooney. Luke pulled Storm up and slid down as he chambered a round in his Winchester. Then he made the call of a Bluejay and waited. No answer. Luke started to worry. He called once more and waited, then he heard a very faint call from not too far away. He looked in all directions and decided there was no immediate danger, so he walked toward the roan horse and Storm followed. He walked up to the roan and patted his neck, and the horse shook his head and snickered.

Luke backtracked the horse and found Rooney lying in some tall grass. Luke could tell that he had dragged himself behind a log for cover and he could see a blood trail in the grass. Luke saw him move and he hurried to the marshal. He saw blood coming from the side of his head and Rooney moaned. It was just a graze, but deep enough to knock him from his horse. Because it was a head wound, it bled like crazy and Luke knew he would have one hell of a headache when he woke up. He tore a 3" strip off Rooney's shirt tail, soaked it in ice-cold water and cleaned and wrapped the wound and Rooney woke.

"How you doin' ol' man?" Luke asked.

Rooney rubbed his head, "Damn, I think I broke my back when I hit the ground, and I got me one giant headache."

"Are you going to be able to ride?"

"Well, I sure as hell ain't stayin' around here. Hey! Ya tore up my best damn shirt!"

"You're welcome. I'll buy ya a dozen when we get back to town," Luke chuckled.

He whistled for Storm, and the big horse turned and galloped to his master, and Rooney's roan followed. The young marshal grabbed his long gun and jumped up on Storm and began looking for the halfbreed's trail. He cut it about thirty yards out on the other side of a water tank and called for Rooney. They rode off to the north. Luke showed Rooney the picture on the wanted poster as they rode and Rooney recognized the crude drawing.

"Holy crap! I put this guy away six years ago for pistol whippin' a whore to death over El Paso way. He has killed a lot of innocent folks over the years and now that I see his face, that mess on the trail from the stage hold-up looks like his handy work, too.

They followed his trail until late in the afternoon and Luke found a safe place to camp by a stream with large boulders they could back up under. The rocks would hold the heat from the fire and protect their back from ambush. Luke walked off into the forest and returned about fifteen minutes later with a hand-full of skunk cabbage and bear berries. He crushed them with a rock to release their healing properties, and placed them in Rooney's tin cup of water that was heating on the fire.

"Holy crap. What the hell are you tryin to do, poison me?" Rooney protested. "Did someone die in this cup?"

"Stop belly-aching. Just drink it down and chew on this," and Luke handed him a large piece of jerky. Five minutes later, Rooney was snoring, his head on his saddle. Luke laid his wool blanket over him and watched him sleep for a moment.

"What a fine man and good friend," he thought. "Thank you for your help, Grandmother," he said out loud. He heard thunder far away, and he knew.

The next morning, Luke had the horses brushed down with handfuls of grass, checked their shoes and made sure they were ready for a hard day. Marshal Rooney rose and was a little confused.

"Luke, what the hell did you give me last night?"

"Are you alright?" and Luke smiled to himself.

"Alright? Hell! I never felt this good before I got shot! Tell yer grandma I said thanks."

Luke smiled, "I already did….Well, get off yer lazy butt and let's go get this back-shootin' SOB."

Rooney saddled up the strawberry roan and they headed back into the thick trees, with Luke in the lead. They were following a trail that only he and Storm could see. Just before high noon, Luke pulled Storm to a stop and looked up towards the horizon.

"What's up?" Rooney asked as he pulled up beside Luke.

"Up there, on the top of the mountain next to that last big tree."

Rooney looked, then squinted and finally saw two figures on horseback sitting perfectly still.

"Are we in trouble?"

"No, it's my cousins, Grey Wolf and White Horse. I'm sure my grandmother sent them to help us get this over with," Luke reassured him.

Fifteen minutes later the two marshals joined the indian riders. Luke found out from them that the halfbreed had turned and headed west, and that he was only about one hour ahead of them; but also that he had joined up with four other indian riders early this morning that were all well armed. The cousins took the lead and moved fast with Luke and Rooney close behind. They had ridden for about an hour and a half when the cousins pulled up just above a large green valley full of tall green grass with a stream running through it.

"We will go around and get behind them," Grey Wolf said as he motioned to White Horse to go to the right as he headed to the left.

Thirty minutes later they were in position, and Luke and Rooney were behind some fallen logs within easy Winchester range. The five men were sitting around a fire drinking rot-gut whisky from their tin cups and laughing. They were all renegades, probably banned from their respective tribes. Their horses had no markings, and they had western saddles, probably stolen.

Luke took steady aim and hit the closest outlaw. The bullet fell a little faster than Luke expected and the round hit the man in the neck instead of the head, sending blood squirting in all directions. He fell backwards off the log he had been sitting on, grabbing his throat and flailing around on the ground. Rooney squeezed the trigger of his Winchester at almost the same time as Luke, and another man fell; both good examples of ol' west law in action. The other three started jumping in all directions trying to find cover and get to their horses. Luke's cousins weren't very good shots from more than thirty yards or so, and they both missed their targets with their first shots. White Horse did manage to wing one of them in the left shoulder, but it only slowed him down. The ramuda of tied horses began jumping and spinning, and some of their reins came loose, freeing them to run off. Grey Wolf was so excited he was firing in all directions without aiming. Luke started to laugh, thinking how glad he was that he and Rooney were out of range, just as a slug from his cousin's rifle buried into the log, inches from Rooney's head.

"Holy crap, is that cousin of yours shooting at us? Or is that your granny's idea of a good time?!" He exclaimed.

Luke just smiled, "I'm not sure but I'd keep my head down until this whole cluster of prickly pears is over."

The three remaining outlaws made it to their horses and headed west with their heads down low. Luke and Rooney stayed down behind the log to keep from catching a bullet from the cousins. When Grey Wolf and White Horse had finished firing, Luke stood and walked down to the outlaws' camp. The man with the neck wound was dead and the one Rooney shot was moaning and clutching his chest in pain, getting ready for his trip to meet lucifer.

Luke whistled for Storm. He slung his Winchester over his shoulder and grabbed his Sharps long gun, mounted Storm and headed west after the last three. He had told Rooney and the cousins to finish up here with the horses, rigs and weapons, and then to head for their village and he would meet them there.

Luke made up ground on the three within a few minutes and he didn't care that they knew he was behind them. He dismounted and laid his 52-caliber long rifle on Storm's back to steady it. He sighted down the barrel and squeezed the trigger smoothly, and the big gun bucked and roared. The saddle bum with the hole in his shoulder now had a hole in his back, about the size of a quarter, and on the front, about the size of a tin coffee cup. The round continued on and hit his horse in the head just between the ears. The horse stumbled into a front flip, throwing the outlaw through the air, head-first into a big pile of rocks. No matter, he was dead before he hit the ground. Luke rode by the squealing horse that was lying on its side, flailing and blowing dust with his nostrils in the dirt. Luke pulled his Colt from his cross-draw holster and put a 45. in the suffering horse's head. He hated to see innocent animals suffer.

Luke rode hard for just a few minutes and Storm had put him in position to take another shot. He slid to the ground opening the breech to his Sharps as he landed. He ejected the spent shell, put a new bullet in and cocked the big gun. This shot was a little longer than the last, maybe three hundred fifty yards, but Luke steadied the long gun on Storm's back, aimed and squeezed the trigger slow and smooth. The gun hammered his shoulder.

He counted, "One, two, three," and the second man fell forward off his horse.

He was just getting ready to jump up on Storm when he got the feeling someone was coming up from behind. He moved behind a tree and watched as Rooney and the roan came up the trail. When he was about one hundred and fifty yards out, Luke and Storm stepped back out on the trail. Rooney saw them and spurred the roan, and they rode up to Luke.

"I should have known," Luke greeted him.

"I can't let you have all the fun; besides, that son of a bitch shot a US marshal, and I'm the marshal he shot!"

Luke smiled, "Is that nag of yours ready to run? That halfbreed knows I'm coming for him, and he's going to wear that cayuse out to get away."

"He's not as fast as Storm, but he'll run all day. He's a good 'un and I won't be far behind ya."

"Okay, let's go get this over with," Luke decided. "Star's waiting for me at the village and I'm ready to be back to my other home."

They took off and Storm reached a gait about two below his full speed, but still faster than most horses could travel for an extended period time. The roan was barely able to keep up. They continued on for about and hour and, suddenly, Luke felt the hair on the back of his neck stand up. He pulled Storm to the left just as a bullet whizzed by his head. He hollered at Rooney to get to cover and he broke off to the right. Rooney pulled his Winchester from its sheath and levered a round into the chamber as he ran for the nearest tree.

"Hey young 'un, do ya see 'em?"

"Yeah," Luke replied. "He's about a hundred and fifty yards out, behind a rock formation to the right of the sun. I'm gonna go 'round to the left. Keep firing about every fifteen to twenty seconds to keep his head down."

"Yeah, I might get lucky and get him with a ricochet," Rooney said hopefully.

"If not, I'll take him from behind."

"You be careful, ya hear?" Rooney shouted.

"I will," Luke said. "Just don't shoot me when I get close".

"Yes Sir, Marshal, I hear ya," said Rooney as he squeezed off a 44.40 from his Winchester.

Luke started his ascent up the mountain through the forest to face the killer in the rocks ahead. He heard the rounds ricochet off the rocks from Rooney's rifle, and he hoped they were keeping the halfbreed's head under cover. He belly-crawled over a very large boulder, fingers crossed that his prey was just below. He was really gonna feel silly if this bad guy got the drop on him. He crawled to the peak of the boulder and gazed down at the rocks below.

"There he was!" Luke thought excitedly.

The halfbreed was crouched down, rifle in his hands, waiting to take a shot down the mountain. Luke stood silently and stared down at the outlaw for several seconds, then spoke.

"I guess it's time we end this."

The halfbreed was startled and he swung his rifle to bear on Luke, but before he was able to squeeze off a round, the over and under, still in Luke's holster, roared and two barrels of lead hit him in the chest, knocking him backward against the rock he had been hiding behind.

Reflex caused him to squeeze the trigger of his Winchester; the slug ricocheted off a large boulder a few feet away and whistled back into his head. He didn't hear or feel a thing. The lead from Luke's shotgun had torn out his heart and he was long dead and on his way to purgatory.

Rooney had collected Luke's long gun, Winchester and Storm, and started up the trail when Luke appeared from around a large rock with the halfbreed's six-gun and rifle in his hands.

"Anything else up there worth checking on?" Rooney asked.

"Nah, it's pretty messy up there, just fodder for the wolves."

Luke found the halfbreed's horse and he was just about worn to a frazzle. His hooves were split and he was lame and would be easy bait for the mountain critters. Luke unsaddled him and he wouldn't leave the area, so Luke walked up beside him and patted his neck and head, and took a piece of hard candy from his pouch and gave it to the worn out animal. Almost overcome with emotion, Luke knew what he had to do. He pulled his six-gun and gently placed the barrel up against the animal's head, sending him to horse heaven; Luke knew there was one.

On the way back, Rooney and the roan tried hard to keep up with Storm. Luke was ready for a good night's sleep, and not on the ground. He wanted to feel Star against his back and to have Bear at the foot of his bed, so he moved along almost faster than the roan could navigate.

It was close to midnight when they reached the Ute village. Everyone that should have been sleeping was up and waiting for Luke. The cook fires were still going and his grandparents, Charging Buffalo and Dark Moon, were waiting for him. Star came running down the hill from where their lodge was positioned on a flat spot. Just as Luke reached to shake his grandfather's hand, she hit him at full-speed, and they both tumbled down the hill another twenty feet or so. Morning Star planted a big kiss on his face, and tears of joy were running down her cheeks. Then Bear hit them both, sending all three rolling.

Yellow Eagle took their mounts and fed, watered and curried them. They found Rooney a lean-to shelter with lots of soft sheepskins and buffalo robes to sleep on. The next morning Rooney found a new set of buckskins by the foot of his bedroll, and they fit perfectly. Luke woke early from the best sleep he had had in many moons and he felt amazing. He and Star rode for three hours before they headed back for the morning meal. By the time they returned Rooney had bathed and put his new buckskins on, and was holding school for the young boys of the tribe, instructing them in the use of firearms.

Two days later they were ready to head home. About sunup, Luke snapped the reins above the mules, Thunder and Lightning, and they were more than ready to hit the trail. They were bred to pull, and pull they did. Rooney was amazed at how much ground they had covered that day. He had never known mules to keep up a pace that fast for that long.

The next day they enjoyed peaceful travel, and rolled into Taos, at just about sundown, Luke asked Star to take the wagons up to the ranch.

"Rooney and I need to stop by the captain's office, and we'll probably have guests for dinner."

Star just nodded her agreement.

They walked into the marshal's office and it was empty. His horse was tied up to the post out front, so Luke's best guess was…the saloon, drinking up his gold coin. Luke, Rooney and Bear walked into the Welcome Inn. Harvy was behind the bar and there were about four tables full of regulars getting ready for the nightly poker games. The captain was leaning up against the bar.

"Welcome back boys," the captain greeted. "Looks like ya made 'er back in one piece, maybe with the exception of Rooney's head."

Rooney blushed and shrugged, "What can I say?"

Harvy served Luke a cold beer, good whisky for Rooney and he poured the captain another shot with a beer chaser.

"Luke, we got a new business in town. I need you to check it out tomorrow and make sure they have all the right documents."

"No problem, Captain, I'll take care of it."

The captain looked at Rooney and winked.

That night, they all dined on beef steaks and mushrooms, sautéed in French brandy, and squash with fresh flour tortillas and butter. Star had canned apricots for dessert with more brandy. Every one slept like a baby that night.

CHAPTER 16

L uke was up and running early. He called Storm, and he and Bear and the big horse headed down the hill to have breakfast with Teddy and Becky. Becky had just taken fresh rolls from the oven and she served ham and eggs and hot coffee with cinnamon. She was amazing in the kitchen. They talked business for several hours, and Teddy showed Luke how the new cafe was very profitable and why.

"Lots of ladies and gents are dining while they wait for their orders of meat to be ready, and Becky's pastries are the talk of the town, he explained.

Becky also made Luke aware of how much she and Teddy loved their new home. Teddy had purchased fifty head of prime cattle and was planning on expanding the herd at Miguel's and the captain's ranches as well. After their conversation, Luke got up and thanked them for a great breakfast and headed off.

Miss Patty Mulvain was an independent business woman and didn't take any crap from anyone. She had a very small waist, very ample breasts and blond hair like spun gold; all natural we presume. She was in her early forties but could pass for twenty-eight or thirty, a very special trait in this hard country. She carried a three-shot pistol in her garter and feared no man.

A couple of laborers were digging post holes and getting ready to set the new sign to advertise as the building was being erected.

Luke dismounted Storm and dropped the hackamore. He spent a few seconds reading the sign and smiled.

"I wonder if I should tell Star we own a whorehouse?" he thought.

He stepped over the wooden foundation and walked out into the area that looked like it might be the saloon. As he was concentrating on the layout he heard a female voice behind him.

"Hey Sweetie, what can I do fer y'all this beautiful morning?"

Luke turned and saw one gorgeous lady standing there.

"We're not open yet, doll face, but I might make an exception in your case. Let's step into my wagon, shall we?"

Luke smiled and said, "Sorry ma'am, but I'm here on official business, I need to make sure you have all the proper licenses for a brothel and a saloon and gambling parlor and anything else you plan on running out of this operation. My name is Marshal Luke Kash, and it looks like I'm your new landlord."

"Well, ain't you just the cutest thing ever," she replied, and Luke blushed. "Ain't never had a landlord that looks like you before. This could be a very special partnership. I got all my papers in order, Marshal. Spent a couple hours at the courthouse yesterday."

Luke liked his new tenant a lot. As they spoke, a slicker in a black suit and starched white shirt with a burgundy string tie and shiny black boots strolled up.

"Marshal Luke, meet my business partner, Charley Prechtl. Charley here will be running the saloon and gamblin' parlor"

Luke shook hands with the dude, and he noticed a bulge under his waist coat over his left rib cage. From the size, Luke figured it was a sawed off belly gun, maybe a Smith and Wesson.

Miss Patty spoke up, "Are ya sure ya don't want a sample of the new business, Marshal? It's on the house, so to speak."

Luke smiled, "It's definitely something to think about, but I wouldn't want to explain to my bride if the news got out."

"Now that's a cryin' shame, Sweetie," Patty replied with a very attractive pout on her lips.

Luke walked off saying to himself, "Bet the other two marshals are having a good laugh about now. Guess I'll wander on over and see."

Rooney and Captain Simms were looking out the window and saw Luke coming. They couldn't help but smile. Luke walked in and Simms innocently asked, "What's up son?"

"Nothing, I was just over checking on my new tenant. Not much of a way her business is gonna fail the way Taos is growing."

Simms and Rooney frowned, "Foiled again. How the hell does he stay ahead of every prank we try to play on him?"

"I think I'll ride out and take a look at the new herd Teddy's putting together, if anyone is interested in riding along."

Rooney looked up, "I'll tag along, since yer new whorehouse ain't open yet," and everyone laughed. They rode out to Teddy's ranch and saw some fine looking cattle. The ranch house was brand spanking new and looked great. They rode out to the pasture and looked close at the cows.

Luke said to Rooney, "Don't look, but we got a rifle pointed at us. It's just over your right shoulder about ten yards back into the trees. When I give you the word, cut hard left to the trees and work your way towards him. I'm gonna head up the other side of the pasture and maybe we can get a look at him before he disappears into the forest….Now!"

Rooney went right and Luke broke left, and headed down the pasture as fast as Storm could go. No one fired as Luke's horse ran a broken path up to the spot where he saw the image in the trees. Rooney rode up just a few seconds later.

"There's signs on the ground that head back into the forest. I'm going to follow and catch whoever had a gun on us. I'll meet you back in town," and he moved Storm up through the pines and after the rider that Luke knew was only a few hundred yards up ahead. Storm picked his way between the tall trees with Bear at his side, and all Luke could do was hold on. The big horse had a sense of whom he was chasing, and he moved ever faster. Luke caught a glimpse of the rider up ahead. He jabbed Storm in the flanks with his heels and the great horse changed gaits and they were flying over fallen trees and burrowing animal holes.

Luke was just about to overtake the rider when they came out of the trees and up to a gate made of logs onto a huge ranch. The swinging sign over the gate said "Casa de Whitley."

Luke knew the name, although they had never met, The Whitleys were the biggest ranchers in northern New Mexico, and KB Whitley was a legend for several hundred miles in all directions. He ran the newspaper in Taos, Albuquerque and Santa Fe, and he owned part of several banks. He had written three or four books on New Mexico and how to survive in the forest without losing your hair to the indians. He had a sense of humor although one look at KB, and you would think he wrote the books after the fact.

The rider busted through the big log gate and jumped to the ground at the front of the ranch house. Luke was shocked when he saw the rider; it was a girl. He slid to the ground and stepped up onto the porch and knocked on the heavy split-log door. KB swung the door open and it swung out instead of in to make it harder for intruders to enter. Luke had to step back to keep from getting hit.

"Marshal, come in." Luke entered the lavish room and they shook hands. The room had bookshelves to the ceiling on two of the walls, and gun racks with shotguns, rifles and handguns of every shape and description. There were paintings of every subject imaginable hanging and leaning against the walls.

KB pointed to a pencil drawing and asked, "Do you recognize this?"

Luke looked and, to his surprise, it was one of his early drawings of Morning Star.

"How did you get this?"

"Your grandmother gave it to me as a gift when I gave her people some beef to help them get through the winter. It's one of my prized possessions. I'm sure your skills have improved since then, but this is still remarkable. What can we do for you, Marshal?"

"I was riding around my ranch and happened to see someone in the trees pointing a rifle at Marshal Rooney and me. I tracked them to your front door."

"Oh really? Would you excuse me for a moment, Marshal?"

Luke nodded and KB disappeared into another room. A few minutes later he returned with a very lovely young woman by his side; very lovely indeed.

"Marshal, this is my daughter, Carol Ann, and I'm afraid she is the one you were chasing through the forest at break-neck speed."

Luke held out his hand, "Very nice to meet you, Miss Whitley."

She blushed some, then took Luke's hand and said, "It's my pleasure, Marshal."

"Can I ask you what you were doing over at my ranch."

"Your ranch? That's the McCracken's ranch," she replied.

"I guess you haven't heard, they were attacked and killed, and their daughter, Maggie, was…umm…."

Carol Ann's breath caught in her throat.

"We understand, Marshal," KB interrupted, putting his arm around his daughter.

"I'm so sorry," Luke said.

She regained her composure, "I have been away back east for several months and I hadn't heard." A tear came to her eyes, "How terrible."

"They were behind in their payments and no next of kin that the banker could find, so I bought their place." Luke felt almost guilty, but not for long. "Well, I appreciate you not shooting me he said."

"Are you kidding? That horse of yours is so fast I couldn't get a bead on you, not even close."

KB broke in, "How about some coffee or maybe some tea? The cook has some sweet bread that I'm sure you'll find to your liking."

They sat at the dining room table and Luke explained how they had caught up with the McCrackens' murderers, and that they won't be hurting anyone…ever again. Luke thanked KB and Carol Ann for their hospitality and stepped off of the porch onto Storm, and they were off, Bear running at their side. He headed west and south, he wanted to give Storm some more exercise and besides he loved being out of doors.

They followed the path from the Whitley spread for a few miles then he headed east for another six or so until he reached the main trail back to Taos. He was about twelve miles out and it was a straight shot back to town. Luke bent down low over Storm's weathers, grabbed a handful of mane and told the big horse to take it on home. Storm jumped and hit the ground running and was at full-speed within three strides. Bear was never more than a few feet behind. What a great feeling, floating on air. Although he had experienced it so many times, Luke was still amazed how smooth Storm was, and the miles flew by. Luke stormed back into town just after noon and the big horse slid to a stop in front of the marshal's office. He dropped the lead next to Rooney's roan and the captain's horse and walked inside. Luke told his partners what had taken place and Simms told him that KB Whitley could be a powerful ally to have.

CHAPTER 17

It had been three months, and Miss Patty's Wild Bush Saloon, Card Room and Gentleman's Sporting Club was up and running. Miss Patty and Charley had done their job of promoting it. They had introduced themselves to everyone in town, to the chagrin of most of the women. They knew full well that if the local women told their men that they better not catch them near that awful place, that's exactly where they would be. And most of the men in town couldn't wait to get into Miss Patty's.

Miss Patty had flyers printed saying "First Drink Free (not to exceed 25cents)" and "$2 credit at the poker tables," and business was booming. Charley had a perpetual smile on his face and he had not had any trouble to mention. But it was just a matter of time, and he and Luke both knew it.

On a Friday afternoon, KB rode into town on a beautiful Palomino stallion looking for Luke. He gave the young boy at the telegraph office a dollar to go to Luke's ranch and ask him to meet him at the Wild Bush. Luke was overseeing the work on a new addition to his ranch house. He was building an office/art studio overlooking the town, and actually the entire valley. Luke told Star where he was going, and she glared at him.

"You keep your hands in your pockets. Do you hear me?"

"Yes, ma'am. I hear you…very clearly." Luke smiled as he rode down the hill, followed by Bear, to meet KB. When Luke walked through the swinging doors of the Wild Bush, things were crazy. A banjo and a piano player were trying to be heard above the noise, and scantily-clad ladies were everywhere, hustling drinks and whatever else they had to sell. Luke took in the whole room and decided it was safe to let down his guard. He walked over to KB who was leaning against the end of the bar, embroiled in conversation with Miss Patty.

"Hey, Lover," Miss Patty said as Luke approached, and KB turned, reached out and shook his hand. Luke just smiled and shook his head at Patty.

"Where's that big dog of yours," KB asked?

"He's sitting on the porch watching the world pass by," Luke replied.

"Can we use your office?" KB asked of Patty and she said, "Of course."

"Would you like a drink, young man?" KB asked as they sat around Patty's desk, Whitley behind it and Luke in a chair in front.

"No Sir, I'm fine."

"Looks like you and me are partners," Whitley said as he took a swallow from his glass. "You own the property and I own the lion share of this business. I have a couple of questions for you."

"How can I help you?"

"Well, you have a very good reputation around the valley for being fair and very generous, and I was wondering if you would like to change our agreement about the rent for a percentage of the profits every month?"

Luke thought about it for a few seconds, then said, "Mr Whitley, you're a very successful businessman. Why in the blue blazes would you want to give some of your profit away if you don't need to.

Whitley, stared at the young marshal for a few moments and said, "Well, I just thought I might tempt you to turn yer head from time to time in our favor."

"My job is to protect the citizens of the United States, and not the rights of the whorehouses of Taos, New Mexico," Luke asserted.

KB smiled and said, That's exactly the answer I was hoping for, my boy. You're a principled man and that's what this country needs. I think we're going to be great friends."

"I truly hope so," Luke responded. "What else can I help you with, Mr Whitley?"

"Call me KB, and I have heard from the trail that there are some very bad men heading this way to do some midnight gathering on your ranches. My guess is they've heard about the quality of your beef and want to tap into your profits."

Luke responded, "I guess they haven't heard what we do to cattle thieves around here, and thats if I don't get to them first because I don't even carry a rope. Do you have any idea when they might be riding in?" Luke asked.

"Tonight or tomorrow night as close as I can tell. That's the thing about progress, it brings along the riffraff with it. I have a few men that are pretty good with rifles if you're interested."

"All the really good breeding stock we keep at the old McCracken place. If that's what they're after, I guess we better give them a greeting. Can you have your hands meet me at the ranch about 4:00 this afternoon?"

"Will do, Marshal." They shook hands and parted company.

Luke told Teddy and Becky to spend the night at his ranch and explained to Star what was happening. She wanted to come along but he convinced her that he needed her at the ranch and she went along with his wishes.

"Thank God," he thought to himself.

He fed and curried Storm to get him ready for a long night. Bear's eyes sparkled and his tail wagged; he knew something was up and he was ready. Luke, the captain and Rooney, along with Bear, all rode out to the old McCracken ranch and arrived just before four. Whitley's men were waiting. Luke recognized a couple of them from around town and shook hands with the five volunteers. KB came around the corner of the new house.

"That's a pretty nice hacienda you have there, Marshal."

"It belongs to my partner and his wife. We had it built after they burned down the McCracken's."

Luke split KB's men up between Rooney and Captain Simms and told them that he was going up the hill a ways with his long rifle, and that no one was to shoot until they got the word from their team leader. Rooney and the captain each took their group in opposite directions around the pasture and took up positions behind cover in order to have the rustlers in a cross-fire; if, in fact, they showed up at all.

It was well after midnight and Luke was just about ready to call it a night when Bear began to growl. Luke pulled his Sharps rifle and chambered a 52-caliber cartridge. The cattle thieves came from the west and south out of the trees, and there were at least a dozen. The full moon lit the pasture along with the fifty or so breeding stock, and Luke was able to see better than most in the dim light. He had the eyesight of an eagle. He waited until they committed to rounding up his cattle before he took aim. He didn't want to shoot any innocents, but Lord help the man that put a rope on his stock. There it was! Two outriders simultaneously threw ropes and pulled a couple of seed bulls out of the herd and headed south with them in tow. The rest of the rustlers started to turn the herd and follow. Luke took dead aim and squeezed off a round and hit the cattle thief on the right. His head exploded, his limp body flew forward off his horse and landed chest-down on the hard ground as the heard was moving his way. Luke had a second round chambered in the long rifle and pulled it tight against his shoulder. The big gun bucked and exploded and the rider on the left was hit behind his right arm. The large round went through his heart and out the left side of his chest, blowing his nipple away, along with a tin-cup-size chunk of flesh. He fell sideways off his mount, dead, as the rest of the herd came his way.

The other ten men panicked, their horses bucking and fishtailing, charging into the herd, which was stampeding and heading south. Right then, Rooney and his men started to open fire from the left and Captain Simms' men started in from the right. Men were falling from their horses and being trampled by panicking hooves. Cowpokes were cussing, screaming and dropping from gunshot wounds and being gored by the longhorn cattle. Horses were going down and their legs were being stepped on by two-thousand-pound animals. It was a frenzy of craziness and horror.

Luke happened to see a glimmer of light come from the trees at the far end of the pasture and he started down the mountain. He dropped his long gun and jumped up on Storm, calling to Rooney to take care of his rifle. The great horse and Bear headed around the left side of the panicking herd, fast after whoever was hiding. Luke assumed it was the boss and he was going to find out.

The pasture was at least two hundred yards square and Luke had Storm running full-out by the time they rounded the frantic herd. Bear had seen the movement in the trees and he was in pursuit. The rustler felt rather than saw his pursuers, and he reined his horse hard right and headed through the trees to make the several hundred yards back to the main trail heading south. Luke slowed Storm and Bear to keep them from injuring themselves by tripping over the underbrush. Besides, Luke knew that once they reached the main trail, it was all over. There wasn't a horse within five hundred miles that could outrun Storm and none that could match his endurance. Luke could see the moonlight shining through the trees and he knew the trail was close.

"Go get him, boy!" and the giant dog was off like a shot.

About fifteen seconds later Storm hit the trail and turned south, and Luke gave him his head. He bent low and held on.

"Lord, this horse can run!" he exclaimed to himself.

It wasn't four or five minutes and Luke saw a horse off to the side of the trail eating fresh grass. Luke pulled up Storm and saw a man limping and trying to move down the trail. He had a six-gun in his hand and he was shooting at Bear. Every time the outlaw pulled the trigger, Bear would move just enough that the bullet would miss its target. Bear looked back and barked, and then moved toward the dark figure. Luke moved Storm slowly down the trail and stayed back about thirty yards until he saw the rustler dry fire his pistol a couple of times. He touched Storm in the flanks and they were off. He took his Winchester from over his shoulder and held it in his right hand and as he rode by the man. He whacked him in the back of the head and he dropped like a big toe sack of turnips. He turned Storm and walked him back to the grounded outlaw and slid off. The man was face-down in a pile of horse dung, moaning and crying.

"Don't shoot! Don't shoot me!"

Luke rolled him over. He didn't want to shoot him in the back. His face was covered in horse dung, but Luke knew there was something very familiar about the man.

"Who are you, Mister, and don't make me ask again!"

"Don't shoot! Don't shoot! I'm Becky's pa!"

Luke looked close and smiled, "I'll be damned! You sure the hell are. I'd have a hard time explaining why I shot my pardner's father, so I guess I'll just let the law hang you."

"Hang me? Are you crazy? Don't you know who I am?" the rustler asked.

"Yes, I do. You're a no-good cattle thief, and the only reason you're still alive is because you're her father, but that won't keep you from being hanged. Luke told Bear to fetch the stray horse, and the man on the ground passed out from the knot on the back of his head. Luke tied his trophy across the man's saddle, not that he was worried about him escaping, but more for the embarrassment of it all as they rode through town…very slowly.

The old man was muttering, "When I get outta this mess I'm gonna kill ya, ya pecker head!"

Luke replied, loud enough for several people standing on the boardwalk to hear, "If you get outta this mess, I'm gonna blow your head off, no questions asked!" And the man shut up.

Two days later just before sunup, Grey Wolf and White Horse were crouched down outside of the ranch house beside their horses when Luke walked out on the porch with a cup of coffee in his hand. He saw them immediately and waved them up. Morning Star and Rosita fixed a huge breakfast and they all talked for more than an hour. The cousins had come to tell Luke and Star that her father, the Chief, had been shot several times in a raid on their camp by renegade horse thieves, and Dark Moon wasn't sure if she strong enough to save him. Luke told the ranch hands to hook up the wagon, but not the ox-cart. They were going to travel fast. Star loaded some supplies in the lodge and they were off. The mules felt the urgency and they moved out at a much faster clip than normal. The cousins were amazed at the speed at which the mules traveled and it was all they could do to keep ahead them. Storm and Bear had no such problem.

About three miles out of town they met Rooney coming back from an assignment up north and Luke asked him to let the captain know that he was traveling fast and would be in touch. Rooney assured him he would. Luke told Morning Star if she felt the need, she could ride Storm and take Bear and hurry on ahead. At first she said no, but the more she thought about it the more it sounded like a good idea. Luke put the pouch with jerky and ammo over her shoulder and slipped the strap for the shotgun over the other one. He whistled for Storm and the big horse came up to her side of the wagon with Bear at his side. She kissed Luke on the mouth, "I love you."

"I know."

She jumped from the wagon to Storm's back, settled herself and touched his sides with her moccasins. The big horse exploded off his mark, almost losing her off his back. Bear barked up at Luke.

"What are you waiting for? Get moving and take care of them!" The monster of a dog busted away from the wagon and up the trail like a shot.

By the time Luke and the cousins rolled into the village it was after midnight and Luke left the team with Yellow Eagle. He knew exactly what to do. Luke found Star and his grandmother and a couple of women from the camp standing vigil over the chief. He opened his eyes when Luke walked in and spoke, "My son, you are here, and Morning Star, too. I feel much better."

"Well I guess we can see who comes first in my fathers eyes,"

Star whispered to Luke, and he blushed, "Sorry!"

S tar and Luke slept until the sun peeked over the horizon. It felt good to just relax in each other's arms. They heard Yellow Eagle leading the mules down to the lake for some water and fresh grass.

Luke scolded, "Hey! Keep it down out there, normal people are trying to sleep!"

"Yeah, yeah," Yellow Eagle replied. "I know what Walks With Bears is trying to do, and I don't believe it is sleeping." And he laughed and moved the stock on down the hill.

That morning after a meal, Luke and Star rode north and east for a couple of hours, Bear at their side. They were enjoying each other's company. At one point they came upon a clearing with three wagons in a loose triangle. They heard singing and shouting and people yelling, "Praise God and pass the snakes!" As they got closer they could see old folks and young people spinning and dancing and holding snakes over their heads.

"What is this all about?" Star asked Luke.

"Some people from the southeast believe that serpent handling is the way to praise their God and gain salvation and glory, but it doesn't make much sense to me. I guess I should warn them about the unfriendly indians in these parts."

Luke dismounted and walked up to the wagons. There was an old bearded man with very few teeth and strange colored blotches of skin on his arms and face. It looked like snake bites and decaying flesh to Luke.

"Excuse me, Mister," Luke took the old man by surprise.

"Hey! Who are you and what d'you want?"

"I'm US Marshal Kash, and you're leaving yourselves open for a lot of trouble being out here like this. Where are you heading?"

"Denver and we're not afraid. God is guiding us."

"Do you know that your God has guided you right into the middle of hostile indian territory?"

"What do you mean? We haven't seen any indians, hostile or otherwise."

"And you won't, either," Luke retorted. "You'll just wake up in paradise. They have been aware of you for the last twenty miles or more, and if they want your stuff they'll take it. They've probably seen you with your snakes and think you are crazy. They think crazy people are a sign from the great spirit, and that may be the only thing that is keeping you alive. If I were you, I would load up, get back on the trail and not stop 'til you hit the next settlement, about twelve miles up."

"You don't need to worry about us, Marshal, we have God on our side."

"The graveyards are loaded with good people that had God on their side." Luke chided as he turned to leave.

Luke and Star headed back down the trail to the village, and about thirty minutes later he felt the trouble. Then he saw the smoke and smelled it.

"I guess I better get back there."

"I'm coming with you," she insisted.

Luke knew better than to argue. He took the lead and Bear ran by Storm's side. Star fell in right behind, her grey working harder than Storm to try and keep up. They reached the sight in just a few minutes but Luke knew it was too late. The wagons were burned to the ground, the horses were gone and the travelers were inside the burning and smoking triangle. They all had arrows sticking out of their bodies as well as gunshot wounds. Snakes were crawling over the corpses in all directions. Luke jumped down and checked around the scene.

He quickly picked up the trail. They were headed west into the forest, and there appeared to be about twelve horses and ten riders.

"Looks like Apaches," Luke said to Star, "by the way they trim their horses' hooves. They sometimes wander this far to raid and take captives. It looks like they may have taken a couple of the children."

"I guess we need to go after them," Star replied as she took her Winchester from her shoulder sling. She checked the chamber for a round then put it back over her shoulder and settled down on the big grey. Luke jumped up on Storm and told Bear, "Find 'em boy, go get 'em." And the beast leapt into action, picking up the trail and they were off. They followed Bear into the forest and he led them at a very rapid pace, weaving in and out of the trees and over fallen logs and stumps without slowing. Luke could see the trail like there had been a herd of buffalo crashing through the woods.

"Go faster, boy!" and Bear barked his understanding. They were traveling through the forest at a speed that only well-trained horsemen could maintain. Morning Star sat her mount and was just two steps behind Luke. He knew she would be right beside him when he pulled up. They rode hard for about fifteen minutes when Bear came to a stop and growled. Luke raised his right hand and Star pulled up beside him. He jumped down and told her to take cover and be aware of her surroundings. He added that he and Bear would be back shortly, and they disappeared into the trees up ahead. Luke walked silently up a rise and then ducked behind an outcropping of rocks as he heard the riders up ahead. He peeked over the rocks and saw the band of Apaches leading two of the stolen horses with two young girls on them. Their hands were tied behind their backs and they had rawhide ropes around their necks to keep them from jumping off their mounts and trying to run off. Tears ran down their cheeks. There were two Apache indians trailing the prisoners about thirty yards back. Luke told Bear to go to the left, while he circled to the right, staying out of sight, and moving quickly and silently through the trees. Over and around rocks and boulders he moved until he was just ahead of the last two captors. He knelt low and waited for the riders to get even with him.

Whistling as he jumped high in the air, he landed with his feet hard against the chest of the indian closest to him, and Bear hit the other with all of his weight. Luke pulled his fourteen-inch fighting knife as he flew through the air, and as they hit the ground he slashed hard with a stroke that almost decapitated the unsuspecting indian. Bear's razor sharp teeth tore at the terrified indian's throat and by the time they hit the ground, his blood flowed at an amazing rate, his life spilling out on the forest floor. Luke made the call of a Bluejay and Morning Star grabbed his long rifle and called for Storm. They rode to meet Luke and Bear.

"We're going to get the girls free, then you take them and head back towards the trail. Bear and I will finish with the Apaches and catch up."

He took his Sharps long rifle from Star and mounted Storm and they headed east. Luke had picked out the spot to confront the rest of the band. He had seen a narrow area in the trail about a mile and a half ahead while he was scouting the last two indians. He and Bear would have to hurry to get ahead. They rode hard for about a half a mile, then he decided to go the rest of the way on foot, leaving Storm with Star.

"When you hear all hell break loose, come riding and shooting," and he and Bear took off running in the direction of the raiders.

Luke and Bear heard the indians before they actually saw them. He pointed to the left and Bear headed up the side of the mountain, and Luke went right. Bear was like a wolf tracking his prey. He passed the raiding party and began making his way down close to the trail. Luke had done much the same thing on the other side and was in position. When the band was about ten yards away Luke stepped out into the open. He levered a round into his Winchester and squeezed the trigger holding his rifle with just his right hand. The lead indian fell backward off his horse and Luke chambered another 44.40 round into his rifle. He squeezed off one more round hitting the second indian on his side of the trail in his left shoulder. A third indian figured out what was going on and charged Luke and knocked him off his feet before he could fire another round. He landed hard against a boulder and almost lost his breath, but managed to cock his Winchester and shoot the fleeing indian in the back of the head. He fell forward off his horse and landed face-down on a large boulder, smashing what was left of his head; dead and gone from this life.

Bear had jumped the first indian on his side of the trail and taken him to the ground. He was face down in the rocks and Bear had his large mouth around his neck. You could hear the bones crack and crunch when Bear bit down. The panicked indian cried out for just a second, passed out then died.

There was nothing but panic and confusion among the indians that were left. Bear leapt into the air knocking yet another raider to the ground and ending his life. Star came riding in from the back of the trail, and she and Luke had the remaining two in a crossfire. The one that Luke had shot in the shoulder was up on his feet and had Morning Star in his sights. Luke had dropped his Winchester when he was slammed against the boulder. He reached down and grabbed the grip of his 20-gauge over and under in his holster, pushed it down and squeezed the trigger in one smooth motion. The sawed off exploded and so did the standing indian's head and part of his left shoulder. A couple of pieces of lead hit the stock of his rifle and splinters of wood flew in all directions as he fell back to the ground—dead, dead, dead.

The only indian left was the one that was leading the prisoners, and Star had her sights on him. She guided her gray around the girls on the work horses using just her heels, and as she pulled up even with the raider, he turned toward her with a bow and a notched arrow in his hands. She lifted her rifle and pulled the trigger at the same time, and a bullet slammed into the rider's head just above the bridge of his nose. He was knocked sideways off his horse and onto the ground, where his own mount stepped on him several times while in a panic from all the excitement and gunfire. Luke looked in all directions, making sure that there were no more raiders hiding in the rocks. He sent Bear out to check as well. He picked up his long rifle then reloaded his over and under and pushed the safety back on. Star had dismounted and was giving comfort to the two girls as Luke walked up.

"How is every one?" he asked.

Star nodded and the girls tried to say they were okay through their sobs. Luke noticed that one of the girls was probably about twelve, and the other was a small but full-grown woman. She was staring into the forest with a strange and distant look on her face. The youngest of the two was more than willing to talk, and rambled on and on about the raid and the indians and what they had done to her parents and the other girl's husband. Luke told Star to feed them and get them something to drink while he policed the area for weapons and horses.

"We need to leave before scouts come looking for the raiding party," Luke alerted Star.

She and Bear lead the two girls and Luke brought up the rear with the four indian ponies that he deemed worth keeping. They were packed with rifles, ammunition and skinning knives. Luke left nothing of value behind, nothing but death.

They motley troop rode into the settlement of Salida about two hours later, and Luke found a preacher man that said he would take the girls to Denver. He said he would try and find them a place to live and a doctor for the older one, even though Luke was pretty sure she was beyond medical help. Besides the trauma of the raid, she also had signs of being bitten many times by serpents.

By the time that Luke and his trusty group made it back to the village it was almost dark and getting very chilly out. Yellow Eagle took the stock to be fed and cared for. Luke and Star found the family and had a very large meal while they spent two hours telling of their exploits. Come to find out, family members already knew most of the tale due to Grandmother's powers and her willingness to share.

The next morning before sunup, Luke and Yellow Eagle, along with Storm and Bear, were off to catch some wild horses. By mid-day they had collected five very nice mustangs, and Luke already had them tame enough to be led by a rope. On their way back to the village, Yellow Eagle asked Luke how he came to be so good with horses,…and dogs?

"It's like you speak their language."

"Some of it I inherited from my father and our people, and some I'm sure is a gift from my grandmother. She seems to be more and more involved in my life as I grow older," Luke explained.

"How is your father, my love?" Luke asked Star as they arrived back at the village.

"He seems to be fine, no sign of anything."

"That's good. Then I guess we better head for home before the bad weather hits. We'll leave in the morning."

She agreed and spent the day with her family. Luke stayed in his grandparents' lodge for several hours. He had many questions that needed answering. By mid-day they were thirty miles from the Ute village, and Star asked, "Can we stop at our spot?"

Luke smiled. She had read his mind.

CHAPTER 19

That afternoon the weather turned icy cold. Luke had just finished catching three very large catfish when the storm rolled in from the west. He dropped the canvas awning and moved the mules, Storm and Star's grey underneath. He tethered the three mustangs as close together as possible on the east side of the wagon. Star had catfish, squaw bread and a pot of coffee, and they hunkered down inside the lodge just minutes before the weather got crazy.

By dark, the wind was howling and the lodge was rocking and rolling; then the hail hit. For almost thirty minutes it came down about the size of apricots. Luke could hear the broncs squealing and jerking at their ropes.

The animals under the cover were faring better, but they were still scared and about to panic. Bear slipped out the trap door and sat under the wagon so that Storm and the mules were aware of his presence. It calmed them considerably.

After the hail came the freezing rain. The damaged roof gave way and the water came streaming in. Luke and Star moved to the back of the wagon and loaded the stove with wood and pulled a couple of buffalo robes over by the fire. Luke opened the trap door and tried to keep up with the flow of water from the treated hides that made up the roof. It was after two in the morning when the storm blew over, and Luke stepped outside to survey the damage. The stock under what was left of the canvas awning were scared but all right; but all three of the broncs were down. Two were dead and the third had open cuts all over its head and shoulders from the hail.

Luke pulled his Colt PeaceMaker and shot the wild horse just below his ear, sending him to sleep forever. Luke suffered more over having to kill an animal than over a human. He had never killed a man that didn't deserve it or hadn't forced his hand.

Luke checked the stock, each leg and hoof; and Bear was still at their side. Luke harnessed the mules, Star's grey and Storm to the wagon to make the load easier for them. He ate a cold meal and hot coffee with Star and they hit the trail.

"Looks like the wolves and grizzlies are gonna eat well today," Star noted

"Yeah, I saw a couple of greys up on the side of the mountain as we were pulling out of camp."

Just then, they heard the wolves sounding the dinner bell.

"At least those good horses won't go to waste,"she agreed.

They rolled into Taos about mid-afternoon—cold, battered and worn, but really happy to be home. The ranch hands saw the wagon coming up the hill and were ready for them when they pulled up to the corral.

"Give them extra feed and curry them, then rub them down with liniment and let me know if you find any problems," Luke instructed.

"Yes sir, Jefe! Do not worry, we'll take care of them."

Rosita had a pot of beans, fresh tortillas and a big cast-iron fry pan of Luke's favorite green chili stew heating on the cook stove. Luke broke out some French brandy and he and Star sat by the fireplace and waited for the meal to be ready. Lord, it was good to be home.

The thunder rolled and it stormed that night, but the mules, the grey and Storm were all safe in their stalls. Bear was at the foot of the bed on his rug. Star was in Luke's arms, and that night they slept the sleep of the young.

Luke was up early to greet the sun, standing on the front porch with a hot cup of coffee in his hand and a heavy wool blanket around his shoulders. He took a deep breath and ice crystals formed as he exhaled. He looked out across the valley that he loved so much, and he thought how his life had changed since that day on the little horse farm where his father lost his life, just a short five years ago. He really missed his mother and father when he allowed himself to think about them. His mother had given him the gift of education, and his father may have given him the greatest gift of all: the ability to survive in the wilderness and to think fast while on the move. Then there was his grandmother, the shaman. What would he do without her? He would have been dead several times over if not for her. She had the Spirit and she gave him the Blood. Bear rubbed up against his leg and huffed and growled his agreement.

Luke had one of the ranch hands take the wagon down to Gunther for repairs and to unload the guns and hardware he had amassed over the last two weeks. He, Storm and Bear headed down the hill to visit with Teddy and Becky, and to partake in the celebration of her morning pastries. Teddy was expecting him and had a steaming cup of joe waiting.

"How is Becky handling the loss of her father?"

"She's okay. She didn't watch him hang, but she was aware of the excitement in town. He was a very hard man and it cost him everything. She's looking forward to talking with you."

Becky came to Luke and hugged him for several seconds, and he saw a tear. She wiped it away and that amazing smile returned to her beautiful face. They sat around a table in the butcher shop/diner, and the hired help waited on the customers that began to trickle in. Becky brought a platter of fresh pastries and a large bowl of butter, and Luke was in heaven once again.

Teddy gave Bear four large bones outside the back door, and they could hear him groaning in ecstasy, crushing the huge bones with his teeth.

"My father was a very rich man and I am his only surviving relative," Becky explained to Luke. "Teddy and I have talked, and we want you to be our partner in my father's property. We trust your decisions and you've done so much for us that we want to continue our relationship."

"I'm flattered. What's going on at the ranch now?" he asked.

"The ranch foreman has everything under control, for the time being, but we're not sure what to do. We don't want to leave Taos and I don't think we can leave the ranch unattended for too long."

Luke thought for a couple of seconds, "Have you checked on the title yet? Did your father owe money to anyone?"

"Just the opposite. My father paid cash for everything he ever did, and he loaned money to lots of folks around Albuquerque. In that respect, he was a good man. He just got greedy."

"Do you want to keep the ranch or sell it and invest the money? Luke asked.

"I don't know how we can run the ranch from here, and we don't really know anyone we can trust to run it."

"If you want, I can ride over and take a look at things so you can make an educated decision, then we can sit down and talk this over again. I'll need you to sign a letter giving me the power to make decisions on your behalf while I'm in Albuquerque."

"Yes, of course. I'll go by the bank and lawyer this morning and have them draw up the proper documents," Becky said and she began to breathe easier.

"I need to meet with Brady and see if he has somewhere for me to be. If not, maybe Star and I can leave the day after tomorrow." Luke kissed Becky on the cheek and shook Teddy's hand and left by the back door.

Gunther and his son had already started stripping the roof off Luke's wagon and checking all the other moving parts. For the most part, the cabin had held up really well.

He told Luke that he was going to triple the thickness of the skins on the roof.

"It will add a little weight but it should be almost indestructible, like the shields I made for the military back in the old country! It may not be completely dry, but it should travel well in two days," he told Luke as he greased the wheels and checked all the joints for leaks.

Luke thanked him and walked into the gun shop to say hello to his friend, Miguel. The old man's eyes lit up when he saw Luke.

"Oh Meester Luke! How are you, my friend? I hear you have been very busy. Are you okay?...and Miss Star?"

"Yes, Miguel, we are fine, but I need some ammunition. How is everything at your ranch going? Do you need anything?"

"Oh no Sir. My wife, she loves the ranch and she has more time to rest. We can't thank you enough, Meester Luke. Life ees very good."

Miguel checked his weapons and gave them a good cleaning as they talked. They were true friends.

Luke left the livery and rode around the corral out onto Main Street. He checked in all directions as he rode. Everything seemed quiet. Hank was moving up the street with his wheelbarrow and scoop shovel, and Luke stopped beside him and asked about his health.

"Oh, I'm doin' purdy good, Marshal. Gettin' through another day."

Luke thumbed a $20 gold coin into the air and Hank grabbed it before it got close to the ground.

"Thank ya, Marshal, I truly appreciate it."

Luke knew it would probably turn into whisky before the next week was through, but that was his choice. "I guess there's worse things than John Barley Corn...like loneliness…bad memories…whatever," Luke mused to himself.

Luke walked into the marshal's office and Captain Brady looked up from his desk and smiled.

"How's my young friend this morning?" He stood and shook Luke's hand.

"I'm doing just fine," Luke answered and took a seat.

They discussed his last trip, in detail. Brady was truly proud to be associated with the young lawman. Luke told him of the situation in Albuquerque with Becky's ranch, and that he wanted to head that way and check things out.

"There ain't a damn thing that can't wait for a week or so, and, besides, you and Star need a little quiet time, so just go on ahead an' go. I'll find ya if somethin' important comes up."

"Thanks, Cap. How's my friend Rooney doin'?"

"He got hisself shot over east of here a day or so back, takin' down a couple of bank robbers, but he's gonna be fine. Maybe a stiff shoulder for a while, but at least it wasn't his shootin' arm."

"Maybe I can get my grandmother to intervene," Luke offered. "I'll see what I can do."

"Can you do that?"

"Well, I can try. I'm gonna hit the trail day after tomorrow, but I'll see you before I go. Ah! Why don't you come up to the ranch for dinner tonight?"

"I'd like that. I'll see ya later on.

Luke walked over to the bank and left Storm and Bear outside the marshal's office. He wanted to arrange a deposit of his grandmother's latest gift into the bank before leaving town.

The bank manager had finally decided he couldn't get ahead of the young man, so he decided to follow his lead and become his ally. Immediately, Mr. Weathers' business affairs began to improve.

"Marshal Kash! How are you this fine day, my friend?"

"I'm doing fine, Mr. Weathers. I have some gold for you to deposit into my account. I'll have Star bring it by after lunch."

He explained Becky's situation to the banker, and that he needed to do whatever necessary to make this as easy on her as possible. Weathers assured Luke that he would take care of the details and that he should probably have an unlimited letter of credit with the bank as well. Luke agreed.

Although he had become a very capable businessman in many different areas, things were getting to the point of being overwhelming. Thankfully, Teddy was proving to be a very confident business manager, and Luke was considering giving him more control over their affairs. This situation with Becky's ranch just helped him make up his mind.

Rooney woke feeling remarkably well. He couldn't figure what was going on, then it dawned on him, "Thanks Luke, yer a good friend." Grandmother had been at work.

Friday morning before sunup, the wagon and ox-cart were loaded with provisions and ready to begin their trek to Albuquerque. Luke had personally checked out the mules, Storm and the grey and deemed them trail-ready. He harnessed the mules and they were off just as the sun was breaking the top of the mountain to the east. It was a frosty morning and the animals' breath reminded him of a steam engine. Star had a buffalo robe to throw over their legs, and they headed down the hill to the main trail and south to Albuquerque.

They passed Santa Fe about four in the afternoon and Luke decided to go a couple of miles further and camp at a spot on the Rio Grande that he knew of…good shelter and lots of grazing for the animals. They rolled into Albuquerque about noon the next day, and Luke checked in with the sheriff to let him know what he was doing in the area. The US Marshal's office was still vacant from the shooting incident over six weeks ago that left the marshal dead in the street. Luke had handled the bank robbers when they rode into Taos, but that still left Albuquerque without federal law, and not too many marshals were interested in the job. The town had a reputation for chewing up lawmen and spitting them out into the muddy streets.

Luke opened the marshal's office and did a check of the interior. Not much left as far as supplies or updated wanted posters. He closed up the office and they headed the three miles south and west to Becky's ranch. They entered through the large gate made out of logs that rose twelve feet in the air and spanned twelve feet. The only words on the gate were "PRIVATE PROPERTY—KEEP OUT!"

Luke drove right on through the gate and toward the very impressive ranch house. Three riders came their way and Luke pulled the team up and waited for them to approach.

"Mister," the lead rider exclaimed, "Yer on private property. Cain't ya read?" he asked.

"As a matter of fact, I'm a very good reader," Luke smiled. "I'm US Marshal, Luke Kash, and I need to talk to the foreman."

This took the rider by complete surprise and Luke could see the confusion in his eyes.

"Uhh…Just wait here. I'll git him for ya."

The three turned and rode back to the ranch house. Luke turned to Star and said, "There's something very wrong here."

He pulled two Winchesters from inside the wagon and laid them between their legs.

"Make sure your shotgun is ready," and she cracked the breech and checked the loads.

Four riders returned; this time the leader was a very large man with a dark complexion full of pock marks. He was riding a big black stallion with a rig that had lots of silver conchos on the bridle and the saddle, and he wore two pistols in black holsters with a black hat pulled down so far it was hard for Luke to see his eyes.

"How can I help ya, Marshal," he asked.

"I'm looking for the foreman," Luke replied.

"Well, yer lookin' at 'um. My name's Bruce Hurtado."

Luke knew the moment he heard the name who he was, Bruce Blue-Eye. He didn't remember the face from the pencil drawing on the poste, but he definitely remembered the name.

Luke played along, "I'm looking for Becky Moore. I have some business to discuss with her."

"And who exactly are you?

"I'm US Marshal, Luke Kash, and I need to speak to the owner of the ranch."

"Well, she's gone off to El Paso for a while; only left a few days ago, so I don't reckon she'll be back for a couple weeks. Is there anythin' I can help ya with Marshal?"

"It's getting kind of late and we've been on the trail all day. Do you mind if we camp over on that grassy knoll? We'll be leaving the morning."

"Not at all, Marshal, make yerself at home. Maybe we can have a drink together later on," he grinned."

"Ya never know," and Luke grinned right back at him.

This kind of unnerved the big man, but he tried not to show it. Luke pulled the wagons up on the hill, unhooked the mules and let them graze. He brought Storm up close to the side of the wagon and laid his long rifle and Winchester under the seat. He made sure his pouch was full of extra ammo, and that Star had plenty of rounds for her shotgun and Winchester next to her in the wagon.

He had pointed the wagon so they could see if anyone left the ranch house. Bear was on watch, making a wide circle around the house. As Luke suspected, they started filing out the back of the ranch house about two hours after dark. He put Star under the wagon and had piled some toe sacks of corn around the perimeter for her protection and to steady her weapon on.

"See the big rock to the left of the road.

"Yes," she said.

"Don't let anyone get closer than that."

"Got it."

Luke had the oil lantern burning in the lodge and the side boards down to draw the riders' attention away from what he and Star were doing on the ground. Seven mounted riders came charging up the hill. Just before they reached the boulder that Luke had pointed out to Star, they started firing. Morning Star opened up with her Winchester and the lead rider fell to his left from his horse. Three of the riders behind him were unable to get out of the way fast enough and trampled him into the trail. Before she could squeeze off another round Luke's long rifle roared from off to her right, and two riders that were in a perfect line from his position, about ten yards from the wagon, were blown backwards off their horses. Star fired again and a fourth cowboy hit the dirt. All of a sudden the three remaining ranch hands weren't as convinced about this venture as they were when their boss gave the order to go root out these folks. They turned and headed back down the hill toward the ranch house. Having reloaded, Luke pulled the trigger smoothly and the big gun bucked against his shoulder. The rider bringing up the rear died instantly. The bullet also hit his horse in the back of the head and they both went down, horse and rider tumbling and ending in a pile of flesh and bone and blood.

The last two riders reached the front of the ranch house and jumped off, letting their horses run free as they busted through the door.

"That's your second mistake," Luke thought as he stepped on the wagon wheel then up on Storm.

"Move down to the big rock as soon as I start shooting."

Star nodded.

Luke gave Bear a hand signal to move out to the left as he went right. He wasn't sure how many more killers were left, but at this point it didn't matter. They were history, and nothing they could do now would save them.

Luke touched Storm in the flanks with his heels and they started down the hill. He had his Winchester in his right hand, moving Storm in a direction parallel with the side of the farm house. As he rode by the first window he saw a dark figure and he fired two shots, almost simultaneously. The glass window shattered, and someone screamed from inside. Star fired two rounds through the front window, and anyone that had thought of coming out the front door immediately changed their mind.

Luke jumped to the ground at the rear of the ranch house and sent Storm out of harm's way. He knelt by the back door and listened; he heard voices inside. Three, maybe four, and one was crying like a baby.

"We're all gonna die! I didn't sign up to be slaughtered like a bunch of wild dogs."

"Shut yer mouth," Blue-Eye said, "or I'll shoot ya myself."

"But were gonna die!"

"Everybody's got to die sooner or later, and he shot the crier between the eyes."

"One down," Luke thought. "Maybe I should just sit out here and wait for them to kill each other off. Nah! What fun would that be?" and he broke through the shaved pine door.

At that exact moment one of the bad guys took it upon himself to charge out the front, completely forgetting that there were no horses for his getaway. He took one and a half steps onto the porch and a 44.40 hit him in the chest, knocking him back against the wall of the house, dead forevermore.

Luke left his Winchester leaning against the rear of the house and pushed the safety off on his over and under with his index finger. He moved stealthily into the building. Taking two steps into the dark room, a bullet ripped through his left arm just above the elbow. It didn't hit any bones, but it sure hurt and really pissed him off. He pushed down on the grip of his shotgun and fired both barrels in the direction the muzzle flash had come from. He heard a man voice.

"God dammit! Ya bastard. I'm gonna blow yer guts out!"

Luke knew the man was hurt, probably mortally, and he said, "I'm here Blue Eye, come on out."

"Ya son of a bitch! When did ya recognize me?"

"When I first saw you, and since I'm part owner in this ranch I was pretty sure you had no business here."

"Well, ya ain't gonna be an owner for long," and he stepped through the door with his two six-guns blazing.

Luke was lying on the wooden floor behind a china cabinet with a prefect view of the shooter. He waited for all twelve shots to be fired and heard Bruce Blue Eye say, "Take that ya goddamn halfbreed. I'll see yer ass in hell!"

"Yes, you will, but I won't be joining you for a while." Luke thumbed the hammer of his PeaceMaker and squeezed the trigger, then fanned the hammer for the second shot with the trigger held back. Two bullets hit Bruce Blue Eye in his blue eye. He spun around and fell to the floor face-down, inspecting the rough hewn pine floor with his good eye.

The next morning Luke walked around the outside of the ranch house and found a mass grave out behind the bunk house. In the main house he found personal items from the real foreman and some of the other ranch hands that had been murdered: clothes, guns and holsters, a cash box with a couple of hundred dollars in it and other odds and ends. He rode into town and brought the sheriff and undertaker with his helper, and three laborers back to the ranch to clean up the mess. Luke took a couple of days to inventory the stock on the ranch, along with all the personal property, so he could tell Becky what she owned.

Luke started to think it might be good to have a source for hybrid cattle to sell to the cities around Albuquerque, and he continued to consider Teddy taking a bigger hand in managing Luke's rapidly growing empire. This was too nice a spread to just sell off. It wasn't about the money anymore. Luke sent a telegram to Captain Simms and Rooney asking if they knew anyone in the Albuquerque area that could manage a ranch this size.

CHAPTER 20

Three days later, he and Star were on their way back home. Luke had taken care of the banking, putting everything that pertained to the ranch in Becky and Teddy's names, and he was satisfied that the new foreman was qualified and would do a good job on his own. It was after noon by the time they hit the trail. They had a good load of Becky's father's personal belongings: a safe and some hand carved wooden boxes that he didn't bother to open, a nice collection of guns of all types and some custom made furniture that would work in Becky's new home. They stopped at the same camp site where they spent the night on the way into Albuquerque. By the time Luke had the mules unhitched and put out to pasture, he could tell that they were in for weather of some kind. The temperature dropped more than twenty degrees in the last thirty minutes. He dropped the awning on the east side of the lodge and brought their horses and the mules undercover. Morning Star had a fire in the stove and a pot of coffee brewing, and she had mixed up dough for squaw bread and soaked some jerky in water along with some dried potatoes to make some hash. Now there was nothing to do except sit back and relax with some French brandy in their coffee, and weather the storm.

Luke was eager to see how the repairs to the lodge would hold up. Thunder, lightning, fierce wind and heavy rain for over an hour, and they were dry and snug…a perfect night for love, not that they had found a bad one. Around two in the morning Bear nudged Luke with his big cold nose. He rose and buckled on his gun belt and tapped Star on her thigh as they snuck out the trap door. They dropped down into the mud and crawled to the river bank. Luke levered a round into his Winchester.

He thought to himself, "There is no good reason for anyone to be on the trail this time of night unless they are looking for trouble."

If that was the case, he would see they got more than their fair share.

Luke and Bear were covered in mud and nearly invisible in the dark of night. He sent Bear downstream to get behind the raiders.

"Be quiet, putos! Ju wan to tell them we are coming?"

Luke could hear them talking, their voices reverberated off the water and he smiled to no one particular. The foot falls of the horses sounded like six as he put his ear close to the ground.

"Mexican bandits! Well okay, let's do this dance so I can get some sleep."

He made a sound in his throat and Storm pulled away from the shelter of the wagon and came to him. Morning Star was at the rear of the lodge with the door open. She had a loaded Winchester in her hands and her 12-gauge shotgun by her side. Luke was up on Storm; he decided to take the fight to the riders rather than wait to be attacked.

The Mexican bandits were about fifty yards out and Bear was just of the trail between the riders and the river, and staying up with them as they moved towards the camp. Luke was sitting on Storm just off the trail as the bandidos came within twenty yards.

He could see they had guns in hand and were ready to attack. Just as the raiders spurred their mounts, the moon broke from behind the clouds and illuminated the black mud-covered figure on the huge horse. Storm reared and then hit the ground running. Luke had his left hand full of mane and his right full of Winchester 1866, and he charged. The Mexicans panicked as they saw the wild figure silhouetted in the moonlight coming straight at them. Luke rode down the left side of the trail at full-speed firing with his right hand. At the same moment, Star began to shoot from the wagon, hitting the first rider on the river side of the trail. The bullet hit him in the head just above the brim of his hat and knocked him backwards off his horse and under the thrashing hooves of the riders behind him.

Luke hit the first rider on his side of the trail in the chest. He slouched and slid off his bucking cayuse. Luke rode straight into the fray and shot a second bandido in the throat. The raider dropped his pistol and the reins to his horse, grabbing his throat, to no avail. Luke didn't have time to cock his rifle so he used it as a war club hitting a rider on his right across the bridge of his nose. Then he hit another on his left on the back of the head. His skull split and blood poured down his back as he crumbled to the ground.

Bear landed on the rump of the last horse in the gang and wrestled the rider to the ground. He bit him on the shoulder and the forearm causing him to drop his pistol. Then he grabbed him by the ankle dragging him off of the trail as he was trying to reach his pistol lying close by. The bandit pulled a knife and managed to slice across Bear's right shoulder and chest before the slashing teeth grabbed his throat and silenced him forever. Luke passed the last bandido and reined Storm around to the left, facing back toward the wagon. He saw Star in the doorway, smoke coming from the barrel of her Winchester, as she scanned from left to right, not finding a target.

He rode slowly up the muddy trail checking each body as he went: one dead, two dead, one breathing. BAM!...a 44.40 to the head, that makes three. Another breathing. BAM!...that makes four. Two more, lying in the mud...dead...6 in all.

Luke walked Storm into the icy water of the river and slid down to wash the mud from his body. He took handfuls of water and cleaned the mud from his horse. He saw Bear walking to the river with his right leg held high; the moonlight showed the blood oozing down his chest, and his heart dropped. Bear fell into the river just as Luke reached him. He quickly washed the mud from his coat then scooped him up in his arms, not even noticing the nearly two hundred pounds of dead weight, and carried him to the wagon.

"I'll take care of him! Don't worry," Star said. "Get the mules harnessed and let's get on the trail."

Luke agreed. When he had the team hitched, he told Star to go on.

"I'll catch up with you as soon as I finish here."

Luke collected the outlaws' horses and guns, and as it turned out, all of the mounts had some worth; so he strung them together with one of the raider's lariats and headed off to catch Star and Bear. They traveled for the rest of the night, and by sunrise, somehow, they pulled into Taos.

Luke pulled the wagon up in front of Doc Burns' office and he jumped down and beat on the door. A couple of minutes later the doc opened up and looked him in the eye.

"You again! Can't you at least have the courtesy to get yourself shot during business hours?" Luke went to get Bear out of the back door of the wagon, and to his surprise, Bear was standing. He jumped down, landing on one front leg and limped into the doc's office and into the back room, like he was going in to bed.

"Check with me after noon, and we'll see what we see."

Luke thanked the doc and flipped him a $20 gold piece.

"That's not necessary Luke. You still have a bunch of credit with merits."

"Okay, then you can buy the drinks this afternoon."

Doc replied, "It'll be my pleasure."

Luke headed the team back down the street to the livery. He tied the Mexicans' horses to the hitching post outside with their holsters hung over the saddle horns and headed up the hill to get some sleep.

Luke woke just after high-noon, dressed and grabbed a cup of joe. He stepped out on the front porch and was almost knocked off his feet; the big dog hit him from behind and then sat at Luke's heel.

"You big ol' pile of bones!" He kneeled and hugged him and rubbed his head. Bear licked his face and rubbed against his chest.

Star came riding up on the grey with a basket of baked goods. "He was coming up the hill as I was going down. It looks like we have your grandmother to thank one more time. The Captain needs to see you when you're up and runnin'."

They had Becky's fresh rolls with butter and honey, and more coffee. Luke whistled for Storm and he came around the corner of the barn and stopped at the hitching post, ready to go.

Luke turned to Bear, "Stay and get some rest."

Bear just turned his head to one side and watched him ride off.

When Luke and Storm were about fifty yards down the hill, Bear stood and started after them with a happy gait to his step.

Luke entered the marshal's office and found Brady going through a stack of new wanted posters, "Hey, my son, how ya doin'?"

"Doin' well, Brady. Had our hands full last night with a bunch of Mexican bandits, but we managed to get through it. Don't know what they were after for sure, didn't really have time to ask. I saw a couple of them hanging around Albuquerque, but don't know if they were independents or working for someone. Anyway, they're unemployed now."

Luke spent the next few days visiting with Teddy and Becky, explaining his plans for the ranch in Albuquerque and they both thought it made sense. He rode with Star and Bear all over the mountain behind the ranch house, even though the weather was turning cold. They all loved being outdoors. Luke had not seen Rooney for several weeks and decided to meet him and the captain at the Welcome Inn for a couple of drinks.

Harvy was excited to see Luke. They had become close friends and Luke always found a way to pay for the improvements around the place. Luke entered the swinging doors and immediately knew something was wrong. He had seen the lathered up horse at the hitching post and figured it wouldn't be hard to spot the owner. He was right. There were two saddle tramps at a table over in the corner drinking and laughing.

"Does that worn out cayuse out there at the rail belong to one of you?"

He already knew the answer, but he wanted to give them a chance to do the right thing

"What's it to you, Squirt?" the dirty, nasty trail bum that had been riding the poor old horse asked.

"You really should get him to the water trough."

"You smart-ass piece of shit! If yer so damn worried about him, be my guest. Oh yeah! Here, take this," and he flipped a nickel into the air.

Luke watched it and let it fall to the floor, "I wasn't looking for a job, I was suggesting you take care of your mount."

"Who the hell are you to suggest anything to me?" The man angered and turned toward Luke.

"Well, first of all, I'm an animal lover and second, it's Marshal Squirt to you."

The saddle tramp turned completely to face Luke and stared him in the eyes. When he saw no fear, he started to back down but didn't want to look yellow in front of his companion and the rest of the men in the bar. He stood and took a stance square to Luke.

"Mister, are you sure this is where you want your life to end?" Luke asked.

The cowboy just looked at Luke confused. "What the hell you talkin' 'bout? You think you can out draw me with that cross draw belly gun?"

"Probably not," Luke replied. "I wouldn't even try with that; but I know I can with this."

He turned enough for the man to get a good look at the over and under 20-gauge in his holster.

The cowboy started to regain his confidence once again, "Are you tellin me you think you can out draw me with that long ol' scatter gun?"

"No, I don't think I can," and the cowboy's grin returned. "I know I can, and I think the last count was thirty-five that felt the same way you do."

"That contraption's over two feet long!"

"That's not your problem," Luke stated. "What you have to decide is, do you want to go take care of your horse or do you want to slap leather and let me give your horse to someone that will care for it?"

"Ya little prick! Ya ain't givin' my horse to anybody, an' I'll kill ya if ya touch it."

Luke's eyes turned black, and the cowboy panicked. He thought he was looking the devil square in the face. The cowboy pulled his gun and started firing before he had cleared leather. The first shot went through the top of his boot and blew his big toe clean off. The second hit the heavy pine plank floor about two feet in front of him; and the third…. Well, there was no third. Luke pushed down on the grip of his shotgun, and the end of the barrel came up level on the other man's chest. Luke squeezed off one shot. It caught the cowboy full in the chest; eight pieces of lead, each one about one-eighth of an ounce. He flew backwards into the arms of his drinking partner who was considering getting into the fray…but not for long.

"Can I do anything for you?" Luke asked the other man at the table.

Violently shaking his head, he replied, "No!"

Luke walked outside and moved the sweaty horse down to the next watering trough and tied him off so he could drink. He knew Gunther and Miguel would be here soon. The dead man looked familiar so he walked across the street to check the latest wanted posters before Rooney arrived.

"Yep! There he is." Luke read, "Javier Aguilar…Wanted for bank robbery, murder, horse thieving…$500 Dead or Alive."

"Horse thief?" Luke thought, "I hope he was better at robbing and murdering than he was at picking out horses, 'cause he was riding a real nag."

He left the poster on Captain Brady's desk and walked back across the street to the Welcome Inn. He stuck his head in the door and acknowledged Gunther and Miguel as they removed the gunman's gear.

"Hey Harvy! Tell the marshals I'm gonna walk down and check on Miss Patty's and I'll be back soon."

"Will do, Luke."

Luke walked the hundred and fifty yards and Bear was at his heel. He sat on the boardwalk as Luke walked on in. Things were jumping. Piano music was playing, shady ladies were parading in very revealing dresses with lots of feathers, and every table was full of cowboys trying to make their fortune, but getting drunk on free whisky instead.

Patty, saw Luke and came to his side. "How you doing, Darlin'? Come to take me up on my offer, I hope."

"It's very generous and I think about it very often; but, truth be told, I'm much more afraid of Star than I am in lust with you. But I promise, if my situation should ever change, you will be the second to know."

"Who will be first?" Patty asked. "I will," Luke replied with a grin, and Patty smiled back.

"Everything okay around here? he asked.

"Yeah, Sweetie, everything is just fine."

As Luke was turning to leave, one of the bartenders approached him with a shot of French brandy. "This is from Mr. Whitley."

Luke had missed him when he came in. He must have been in the back office. He excused himself and walked over to shake hands with KB, and they each downed their drinks.

"How are you doing, Marshal?" KB asked.

"Doing just fine, Mr. Whitley, and how is that lovely daughter of yours?"

She's doing fine; settling in to ranch life. There's not much for a young lady to do, but she'll be okay. Do you have a few minutes to talk some business?" KB asked.

"Sorry, Mr. Whitley, I have a meeting with Captain Simms. Maybe another day. When will you be in town again?"

"How about Friday morning at the butcher shop? I've heard they serve an incredible breakfast." KB said.

"Yes Sir, I'll see you there 'bout an hour after sunup?"

"That will be fine, Luke, I'll see you then."

Luke turned and left Miss Patty's. He and Bear walked back down the main street of Taos. Luke walked into the Welcome Inn and bellied up to the bar beside Rooney and the captain.

"Hello, gentlemen," Luke greeted his two friends.

"Howdy, Luke." Rooney reached out and shook his hand, and Brady did the same. They had been standing and talking for about thirty minutes when one of Luke' ranch hands staggered through the swinging doors and collapsed on the floor.

"Meester Luke, they shot Rosita and took Miss Star," he managed to mumble before he passed out.

He had two bullet wounds, one in his belly and another in his chest, between his heart and shoulder. He died before Luke could get anymore information from him.

"Rooney, get Doc Burns headed up to the ranch."

"I'm comin' with ya," Brady insisted, and they all ran out the door to their mounts.

Luke was up on Storm and off towards the ranch before Captain Simms had untied his horse. Storm sensed the urgency in Luke's demeanor and ran faster than ever up the hill. He skidded to a stop in front of the long porch. Rosita was lying face down with blood oozing from under her, and running between the planks of the porch. She was breathing but incoherent and she mumbled in Spanish. Luke put his hand on her head and silently spoke to his grandmother and asked for her help.

Brady Simms was a full two minutes behind Luke, and came riding up as Luke was coming out of the ranch house door. He had his Sharps long gun in his hand and jumped up on Storm. Bear was turning in circles and barking, sounding like a great animal of some unknown kind.

Luke told the captain, "Looks like there were five of them and they dragged her off at the end of a rope. See what you can get from Rosita when the doc gets here. I'm headed up the mountain after them."

"We won't be far behind," Brady said.

Storm and Bear headed away from the ranch at full-speed with Luke bent low over the great horse's neck. It wasn't hard for Luke to follow the raiders over the pine needles and leaves on the forest floor. There was also a blood trail and Luke's heart sank as his temper rose.

"You bastards, you're already dead! But if she is hurt, you will suffer the most painful deaths imaginable, I promise!"

The threesome charged up the mountain for over thirty minutes and almost over ran the bandidos. Bear jumped and slid to a stop and Storm pulled up hard. Luke jumped down and headed to a large rock for cover. He pulled his long rifle from its soft deerskin sheath and quickly slid a 52-caliber round into the breach and closed the lever. He peeked over the large boulder and saw five men standing around in a circle in a draw about three hundred and fifty yards down the trail. He saw Star tied to a tree. She looked bloodied and her clothes were torn and tattered. One of the men approached her and said something, then slapped her face. She turned her head and then kicked him in the crotch. He went down hard on his knees and Luke couldn't help but smile at her spunk. Before the cowboy with the wounded manhood could regain his composure, Luke put a large bullet into his shoulder. A second raider by him went down from another one of his shots. Luke picked his next target as he reloaded the Sharps. He didn't want to deliver any fatal shots, as he intended to deal with each one of the saddle tramps personally.

Bear was just reaching the site of the kidnappers and flew through the air, knocking two unsuspecting men off-balance and hard to the ground. He bit each one hard on the legs and arms, disabling them to the point that they couldn't escape. Luke squeezed the trigger and blew the right knee out of the fifth raider standing. He cried out and went down, flailing around on the ground as blood spurted in all directions.

Luke mounted Storm and headed down the hill to confront the band of outlaws and to free his bride. He dismounted and laid his long gun against a tree. He ran to Star and she tried to smile, but was very weak. She screamed. Luke spun around, pushing the safety off of his over and under as he went; his peripheral vision picking up the man without a kneecap holding a six-gun and trying to train it on Luke and fire. From eight feet, the two barrels belched sixteen chunks of lead and almost blew the man's head to pieces. Shreds of skin and an eye ball hanging down, the torso fell flat to the bloody ground. He broke the breach and replaced the two shells then pulled his large fighting knife and cut Star free. She fell into his arms and he lowered her carefully to the ground.

"Are you okay, my love?" She nodded.

Luke walked over to the first man with a bullet in his shoulder and asked him, "What were you thinking kidnapping a US Marshal's wife? Are you nuts?"

"We thought you 'er rich and you'd pay anythin' to get her back."

"Well, you were right about that. I would pay anything to get her back, if you weren't so stupid."

Luke pulled his PeaceMaker from his cross-draw holster and shot him in both knees to bleed to death. He walked over to where Bear had the last two under his control. He tied them to a tree and then cut the tendons just above their heels so, if they should get loose, there would be no way they could run. Luke went back to check on Morning Star and he talked to his grandmother as he walked. He felt a warm calming presence come over his body and he knew she was with him. He sat on the ground beside Star and they rested for several minutes. He could see her regaining her strength.

Luke gathered the kidnappers' horses and rigs and collected their holsters and side arms. He put their rifles in the sheaths on their saddles.

"Do you feel up to riding?" he asked.

"Yes. That will be a lot better than the way I came up the mountain," she answered.

"Yeah! Dragged behind a horse should always be your very last option when you're choosing a way to travel." He gently kissed her forehead and pulled her in close, hugging her longer than a minute before letting her go. He gave her a boost up on one of the outlaw's mounts. They were just about to head up the trail when one of the men tied to the tree began to holler.

"Hey! You can't leave us like this. We'll bleed to death!"

The other one chimed in, "Yeah! Cut us loose! Please!"

Luke turned Storm and moved him in front of the two.

"You're right, I can't leave you like this," and he pulled his Colt PeaceMaker from his cross-draw holster and shot them both between the eyes. They slumped forward, still tied to the tree. Luke jumped down from Storm and pulled his fighting knife from the sheath behind his holster and cut them both free letting them fall to the ground.

"Sorry. I couldn't wait around to watch you start your journey down to lucifer. This way we will all be satisfied."

He jumped back up on Storm and caught up with Morning Star and Bear and they headed up the trail toward home. They had only gone about a quarter of a mile on the trail to home when a shot rang out. He heard Star moan and fall from her mount. Panic ran through his body and he jumped down from Storm and ran to her side. A large bullet hole in her chest was oozing an enormous amount blood. He put his hand over the wound and applied pressure, to no avail, since the bullet had gone all the way through. Life was pouring from her body. Luke knew there was only one thing he could do. He grabbed her up and held her tightly. Just as he started to call for his grandmother's help, a bullet ripped through his body, entering under his right shoulder blade and exiting his chest, just missing his heart. The bullet continued on its path, hitting Star just below her rib cage, puncturing her liver. Her blood began to run black.

CHAPTER 21

Luke woke up in his bed at the ranch with Doc Burns sitting in a chair by his side. It had been two days, and he was trying to clear the cobwebs and piece together what had happened when he finally remembered being bush whacked.

"How is Star?" He tried to sit up, without much success but with plenty of pain. He groaned.

"Luke, just lay back and relax; you're lucky to be with us. It's all we could do to keep you alive. Your grandmamma must have used every ounce of power she had. I have never seen anyone wounded as bad as you make it, especially traveling down the mountain they way we did. If that dog of yours hadn't come and found us, you would have died for sure. Just rest for a bit."

"But what about Morning Star?"

The doc got up and left the bedroom just as Brady Simms came in.

"Brady, what's going on? Where's Star?"

Bear moaned.

"Do you remember anything about the attack on you and Star?" Brady asked.

"I remember she was hit and I jumped down,… then… I don't remember much after that."

He tried to focus but couldn't come up with anything.

"You were shot and it was all we could do to keep you breathing while we got you home. The ol' lady must have been watching over you."

"But what about Star? How is she?"

Brady hung his head, "She didn't make it, Luke. She was already gone by the time we got to you. I'm so sorry."

Tears came to Luke's eyes and although he didn't sob out loud, his heart was shattered into millions of tiny pieces. At that moment any compassion he had ever had for people that broke the law completely disappeared.

"Captain, can I be alone for a while? Luke said in almost a whisper.

"Sure thing, my friend," he said and turned to leave.

"Hey, do you have any information on the bushwhackers?" Luke asked as Brady got to the door.

"Yeah, we do. I'll have it all ready for you when yer up and about."

Luke felt someone put their hand on his head, and he heard himself say, "Grandmother what happened? Where are…?" and then he drifted off to sleep.

Two days later, Luke woke at sunrise, dressed and went down stairs. Rosita was in the kitchen and she came to Luke and gave him a big hug.

"I'm so sorry, Meester Luke," and tears came to her already red, swollen eyes.

Her left arm was in a sling and she handed him a cup of coffee.

"Can I fix you something to eet?"

"No Rosita, I'm fine. You need to get some rest. I'm going into town."

He was still very stiff but, surprisingly, there wasn't a whole lot of pain. He whistled and Storm came from the barn and skidded to a stop in front of him. He stepped up on the hitching post and mounted Storm. Bear barked very loudly and the threesome headed down the hill to town. Luke rode on by the livery and headed south to Brady's ranch. As he rode up the trail he saw the captain saddling his horse. He was totally surprised to see Luke out of bed.

"I'll be damned. You're a complete amazement to me, son. I don't understand any of this, but I'm glad yer okay."

"Thanks. Follow me to the butcher shop and I'll buy you breakfast."

"I'm right behind ya," said Brady.

Luke turned Storm and headed out to the main trail at a fast gallop. They both reined up in front of the butcher shop at the same time. Becky and Teddy were putting out the "open" sign and unlocking the front door. Their two employees had been butchering and checking on meat in the walk-in smoker since four o'clock that morning. There was a large number of fresh pastries in the display case that Becky had prepared the afternoon before.

Luke, Brady, Teddy and Rooney sat at a table and had coffee and baked goods while they waited for Becky to prepare their food. It was hard for them to strike up a conversation; no one wanted to bring up the loss of Morning Star.

Luke broke the ice, "My friends, you don't need to pussy foot around, I have come to terms with Stars passing. But I hope that none of the people involved are friends of yours, because they are all dead. I just haven't informed them yet. Brady, can you tell me what you turned up?"

"Yeah. The people that took Star worked for a bad hombre named Jesse Good, from over Fiddler's Bow way. They were already gone by the time we arrived and it was all that we could do to get you back alive. I just received new posters on them two days ago. Looks like you took care of all but four in the gang. They are all wanted, dead or alive."

"Well, I can guarantee they won't be coming back alive, and if any of you are squeamish, I'd stay here till I get back."

"I'll be riding with ya and yer in charge," said Rooney.

"Do ya wan't me to come along?" Brady offered.

"How many did you say were left in the gang? Luke asked.

"Just four."

"I'm pretty sure Rooney, Bear and I can handle four killers. I'll meet you here tomorrow morning about an hour after sunup," Luke told Rooney and got up to leave just as KB Whitley and his daughter, Carol Ann, came through the door.

Carol Ann walked over and gave Luke a big hug without saying anything. She looked him in the eyes and saw the pain, and she stroked his cheek with a soft hand. KB reached out and shook his hand, "I'm so sorry son."

"Thanks, Mr. Whitley, I really appreciate it."

That afternoon they buried Star at the ranch by the stream that ran into the pool under a large oak tree. Her father, the chief of the Ute nation, her mother, along with Luke's grandparents, uncle and cousins were all in attendance; along with just about everyone in the valley. The townfolk brought food and drink and it was a very somber occasion, but Luke tried to cheer everyone up by telling stories about what an incredible person she was, and how he would always be grateful for having had her in his life.

Shortly after dark, Luke, Teddy, Brady and Rooney were sitting in the rockers on the porch with Bear at their feet, drinking French brandy. They drank several bottles and everyone had a tear come to their eye, except Luke. His eyes were turning black, the way they did just before he pulled the trigger on someone that braced him. They weren't going to turn back. Black would be the new normal for him.

The next morning Luke and Rooney met in front of the butcher shop. Luke had brought Star's gray for Rooney. It was the only horse within five hundred miles that could come close to keeping up with Storm. They had a good breakfast and Becky packed enough meat and baked goods to last them several days.

Fiddlers Bow was a small town about seventy-five miles north and east of Taos, originally founded because of gold. As it turned out, some placer gold was found but very few veins or strikes came to fruition. Now it was more of a hideout for shady characters, horse and cattle thieves, bank robbers and anyone trying to evade the law. Unfortunately for them, the law was aware of their location and on their way.

It wasn't quite the dead of winter, but it was cold and it looked like it might snow at any moment. Luke was dressed in his buckskins with a light-weight leather coat but he didn't notice the cold. He was completely focused on the task at hand. He had a heavy wool blanket hung over Storm's withers, his pouch full of ammunition and food, his Winchester slung over his shoulder and his Sharps long rifle in its sheath across his thighs.

Rooney was provisioned up with saddle bags full of ammo and food and a heavy sheepskin coat lashed to his saddle. He had his Winchester in a sheath under the right flap that held his stirrup in place over his cinch.

"What do ya call this horse?"

"We call it Gray," Luke replied without emotion. "We just kept it simple."

He touched Storm in the ribs with his heels and the big horse moved out to a fast gallop, and the gray stepped out to keep up with Storm and Bear. They took the trail that ran to the northeast and rode 'til after sundown. Luke wanted to get this over with. They camped at a spot Rooney knew of by a clear stream. They built a fire and had coffee and baked goods and smoked meat. For being away from home, it wasn't too bad. Luke leaned against a log with his wool blanket around his shoulders and ignored the cold, his black eyes staring off into the dark sky. Bear laid beside him. Rooney used his saddle as a pillow and laid on his horse blanket, covering himself with his heavy sheepskin coat, teeth chattering. He almost froze all night, and the night was long.

The next morning Luke added more coffee to the pot and more water along with what was left over to make a new pot of joe. They ate some jerky and some of Becky's pastries, and they were off.

Rooney broke the morning silence, "We traveled about fifty miles yesterday, and at that rate we ought to be in Fiddler's Bow by around noon."

Luke wasn't much company on the ride. He was looking straight ahead and pushing Storm to go faster and faster, and the big horse responded. It was just before high-noon when they hit town and looked for the local lawman. They found a small building that said, "Sheriff's Office" but the door was locked. They looked around and saw the saloon and Luke motioned to Rooney. They headed across the street to check in with the town gossip—the bartender.

"Let me go in first and check things out. I'll signal you."

Luke walked through the swinging doors and into the bar room. He looked around then walked up to the bar.

"Any law in this town?"

The bartender pointed to a table in the corner. Luke had seen the man when he walked in, and he seemed to be sleeping. He still was. Luke signaled for Rooney to come in then he walked over and kicked the chair the sheriff was sleeping in.

"What the hell!" the sheriff said, as he was startled and tried to focus on what was happening.

"Are you the sheriff?" Luke asked.

"Yeah ! Who the hell wants to know?"

"US Marshals Kash and Rooney. Is this where you live?" asked Luke.

"Uh…no…Uh…sometimes, I guess. What can I do fer ya, Marshals?"

"Where can we find Jesse Good?"

"I s'pose his ranch would be as good a place as any to start looking," replied the sheriff.

"And where would that be?"

"About two miles east of town."

"Let me ask you a question. Have you seen any of the newest posters?"

"Of course I have!" said the sheriff.

"Then why aren't Jesse Good and his boys in your jail or dead?"

The sheriff just looked at Luke, trying to find the answer the marshal wanted to hear.

"Uh…uh…umm…."

"You need to get over to your office and get ready to receive some prisoners. Do you understand?"

"Yes, Sir, Marshal. I do, and I'm on my way," the sheriff replied, and he rose from his chair and left the bar.

Luke walked up to the bartender, "Buy the sheriff a couple of good whiskys if he's still around tomorrow," and he flipped him a $10 gold piece. "Do you have any idea how many men Jesse Good has with him?"

"He had nine living out at the ranch, but five of them have disappeared. Haven't been around for a week or more."

"Yeah, well I wouldn't be looking for them anymore if I were you." Luke related the story to him, "They've gone to meet their maker, or somebody. Is there anything else we should know about Jesse Good?"

"Only that he's a real mean hombre and he'll put a bullet in yer ass in a heartbeat."

"He, or one of his gang, already has and now he's going to pay for it with his hide; and God help anyone that gets in our way."

R ooney, Bear and Luke headed north on the trail out of town and stopped about a quarter of a mile from the ranch where Luke knew Jesse Good was holed up. They reined their horses into the woods.

"What's yer plan, Marshal?" asked Rooney.

"I'm thinking about walking up and knocking on the door and blowing the hell away whoever is stupid enough to open it."

Rooney wasn't sure if he was serious, but thought he just might be, so he waited for orders.

"I'm going to take Bear and get around back. You get as close as you can without exposing yourself, and cover the front."

"You got it," Rooney replied.

Luke jumped back up on Storm and headed through the trees with Bear at their side. He pulled up behind the corral and dismounted. He dropped the lead rope to the hackamore and he started toward the house with Bear at his heel. About twenty yards from the back of the ranch house, Luke saw something shine in the window. He and Bear jumped for cover behind a pile of firewood just as bullets started flying. He heard Rooney start shooting and the gunfire coming his way started to calm. He unslung his Winchester and peeked over the corner of the wood pile. Firing two shots through the window at the back of the house, he sent Bear out into the trees to work his way up closer. Luke put two more bullets in the rear door to break the latch and, just as he was hoping, the door splintered and swung inward. Rooney saw Luke move from the woodpile and head toward the back of the house, so he stood up and headed for the front, firing as he went. The door opened and one of the gang started out. Rooney put a 44.40 in his chest and he went down, partially blocking the doorway.

Luke saw a dark figure at the rear door and he fired two rounds. He heard a yell.

"Ya sons a bitch! I'm gonna cut yer balls off," and a very large man busted through the door wearing nothing but a flannel shirt and boots, with two six-guns blazing.

All of a sudden, a black storm cloud came rushing in over the area. Heavy winds began to blow and the temperature dropped twenty-five degrees to well below freezing. Luke sat down on the ground and closed his eyes.

He heard Star's voice and he was frozen in place, unable to move.

"My love, I am with you. I will always be with you. Have no fear, your grandmother and I are here"

Luke tried to contact her with his mind, but there was no answer, only the words he had heard her speak. He opened his eyes not knowing how long he had been oblivious to his surroundings. He saw Bear almost suspended in mid-air, and the outlaw seemed to be frozen in his tracks. It was almost as if time was at a stand still. Puzzled, Luke blinked and shook his head, and everything came to life once more.

Bear hit the large man from behind and knocked him forward to the ground. Luke moved up and kicked his guns away and hit him hard in the back of the head with the butt of his Winchester. He lost consciousness, and Luke and Bear started into the ranch house. Just as they were entering the back door, shots rang out from inside, and Luke and Bear backed away and cozied up against the outside wall.

Rooney had made his way to the front porch and kicked the gun away from the dead man's hand, then peeked through the door.

"This is US Marshal Rooney. Come on out with yer hands up and you might get out of this alive. But if you make Marshal Kash come in after y'all, yer time on God's green earth is up; mark my words."

"Why don't you come in and get us, Marshal!" came a voice from inside.

"Well, I guess that's an option, but it's one you won't like the outcome of. Let me ask ya a question. When was the last time ya sat beside a stick of dynamite when it went off?"

Rooney tossed a twelve-inch-long branch through the door. It hit and bounced around the room. Someone inside yelled, "Dynamite!" and Rooney heard footsteps running for the back door.

He stepped inside and fired two quick shots with his Winchester, then hollered, "They're comin' yer way, Luke!"

Luke stuck the barrel of his rifle across the door jamb just as the first of the two men came barging through. He tripped and landed on his face, and the second man stepped on his back and went down. Bear jumped and landed hard on his back. As the first man tried to get up, Luke smacked him across the bridge of his nose, and he went back down, out cold.

"All clear, Rooney. Come on out and give me a hand," Luke called out.

"Which one is Jesse Good?" Rooney asked.

"I'm guessin', the big one over there with the smashed in nose and no clothes."

Rooney walked over and studied the big hombre spread out on the ground.

"Luke, you know anything 'bout these scars all over his body?"

"Yeah, a little. There's an indian tribe down in Mexico that burns symbols into their skin with red-hot irons, kind of like branding. It's a religious thing. Some of them go crazy from the pain. My guess is he's one that did."

"Why are these guys still alive, if ya don't mind me askin'?"

Luke just looked at Rooney with black eyes and a faraway stare, "I want to watch them hang, long and slow. Let's get them bound up and on their horses."

They rode into Fiddler's Bow, leading four horses with three live outlaws, and one dead, tied across their saddles. When they were about fifty yards from the sheriff's office, it went up in a huge ball of flames and a large explosion. Storm shied away from the blast, but Luke quickly got him back under control and kept the other horses from panicking.

Jesse Good began to laugh, "Whaddya think of that, Marshal?"

Luke replied, "I think your even dumber than you appeared to be in the beginning, because instead of hanging you, I'm just gonna shoot you!" And he pulled his Colt PeaceMaker and put a bullet in the big man's butt.

"Okay, I changed my mind. I'm not quite ready to see you die just yet."

"Oh, you sonsabitch! Get me to a doctor."

"I don't think so," Luke responded. "I'm not sure I'm through puttin' holes in you yet. I will guarantee one thing: You won't be walking away from this," and he shot him in his right foot.

"Aaah, goddammit! When this is over, I'm gonna kill ya!" and Luke shot him in the other foot.

"Hey! You can't do that! Yer a lawman," one of the other outlaws yelled.

"Right now I'm just a pissed off husband," and he put a 45 slug in the man's knee.

"Whatever chance you had of getting out of this just went up in flames…literally."

Bear growled, and Luke turned toward the end of town and saw two riders running hard for the trail east. Luke told Rooney to take care of the captives.

"And if they're dead when I get back, I won't mind."

He and Bear headed out of town at a dead run. Storm could feel the urgency in Luke's body and he ran like the wind, Bear matching him stride for stride. By the time they passed the last building in town, they had already made up ground on the bombers. Luke bent down low over Storm's shoulders and let him run. The trail was lined with tall pines and giant oak trees, and it was like Luke was floating through a tunnel. He closed his eyes and heard Morning Star's voice.

"I'm here, my love. I'm with you."

Thunder crashed and lightning flashed, and when he opened his eyes, he was within fifty yards of the riders. One of the saddle tramps turned and looked back with surprise on his face. He said something to the other rider and they split up.

Luke motioned, and Bear understood, running off into the trees after one of the riders. Luke continued on the trail after the other, trying to decide how he would deal with him. He settled on counting coup, the indian way of showing superiority over an enemy by getting close enough to touch him with a coup stick; in this case, a Sharps 52-caliber buffalo rifle.

The rider pulled his six-gun and began to fire around his left side, with little or no chance of hitting anything but the ground as he bounced in the saddle. Luke moved Storm to the right side of the trail, so there was no way the outlaw would have a shot. When the shooter turned back to the right, Luke moved Storm to the left. After six shots, the outlaw tried to replace his pistol in his holster and missed, the six-gun falling to the ground in the middle of the trail. Luke ran Storm up against the left side of the fleeing man's horse. He reached out with his long rifle and touched him on the left shoulder, then he touched him on the right shoulder, then he drew back his rifle and swung it with all his might, hitting the man beside his right ear, knocking him unconscious. He collapsed and slid off his horse landing on his head, breaking his neck. Luke left him lying, limp and very dead, in the middle of the trail.

He pulled Storm up and turned him back the way they had come to find Bear and the other rider. He picked up the lead of the dead man's horse and had gone about a half a mile when he saw Bear leading a horse out of the trees and onto the trail. He pulled up beside his dog.

"Is he dead, boy?"

Bear barked, and they continued on back toward Fiddler's Bow.

When they rode in to town, Luke could tell something was wrong. Star's gray that Rooney had been riding, was wandering loose in the street. Luke rode on by, then went around back of the saloon and dismounted. He unslung his Winchester and levered a round into the chamber. He moved slowly to the back door and paused. He could hear voices coming from inside the saloon.

Luke snuck silently into the back door and saw the body of the bartender lying stone cold dead in the store room. He heard noise in the kitchen area and he drew his prized fighting knife from its sheath. He came up behind an outlaw trying to get a fire started in the cook stove and reached around with his left hand, covering the mouth of the saddle bum. Luke slit his throat with one swipe, almost to the point of beheading his victim, and he let the body slide slowly and quietly to the floor.

Luke backed up against the kitchen wall when he heard one of the outlaws coming his way.

"Randy! What the hell ya doin' in there? We're all hungry, get a move on!

There was nothing but silence from the kitchen. "Randy?...What's goin on?"

He walked into the kitchen and Luke took his head off with a deadly blow from behind. He crashed to the wood floor, blood streaming from the headless body by the bucket-full. Luke wiped his blade clean on the dead man's shirt and slid it back into its sheath. He stepped into the doorway and looked around the saloon. He saw Rooney lying face down on the floor, three bullet holes in his back. Jesse Good was sitting in a chair with both legs up on another, bandages on the wounds that Luke had inflicted. He was trying not to put any pressure on the bullet hole in his butt. The other outlaw was on his feet using the back of a chair to brace himself while he looked out the window to check the street.

Luke sent Bear at the man by the window, and he brought his over and under 20-gauge to bear on Jesse Good. Bear's sharp teeth sunk deep into the back of the man's thigh and he dragged him to the floor. He ripped and tore flesh from the man's leg and then moved to his right arm as he tried to reach for his six-gun. Luke could hear bone crushing under the pressure of the great dog's teeth, and the outlaw screamed in horrible pain; but only for as long as it took Bear to move to his throat and break his neck with his powerful jaws.

Luke stood in front of Jesse Good and stared him in the eyes.

"How many damn lives do you have?" Good asked him.

"At least one more than you," and Luke pulled both triggers on the shotgun in his holster and Jesse Good's head disappeared in a flash of blood and bone. What was left of his corpse tumbled over backwards and sprawled out on the rough-cut pine plank floor, his Spirit and his Blood, on its way to where ever people with a soul like his go.

Luke looked outside and the snow was beginning to fall. He fixed Bear and himself a good hot meal, and then gathered up the weapons that would sell and loaded them onto the outlaws' horses. He walked to the mercantile to provision up. No one was around; in fact, it didn't look like anyone had been around for quite some time. He grabbed a heavy coat, some gloves, a couple of cans of peaches and some jerky. He looked at the dried meat.

"I won't leave town without my wagon and Teddy's good smoked meat again; and I won't let my emotions rule my actions ever again."

Luke looked around Fiddler's Bow and realized that no one but outlaws had inhabited the town for a long time. He took the time to pour four cans of coal oil over the buildings and light them on fire. He waited just outside of town to make sure every building was burning, then he, Storm, Bear, the gray and the outlaws' horses headed southwest down the trail.

The weather was turning bad, and Luke should have gone straight to Taos and home; but when he came to the trail that headed northwest toward his people, he turned Storm and bent low over Storm's shoulders and closed his eyes. Luke heard Morning Star's voice.

"Be strong. I'm with you."

He heard his grandmother's voice saying, "I'm here, my son."

When Luke opened his eyes, he was in the Ute village, and his grandparents were standing by Storm's side. Yellow Eagle was there and he took Storm and the other horses to shelter and Bear followed. Luke went to his grandmother's lodge and collapsed on the pile of buffalo robes that he always slept on.

Luke woke about mid-day, his grandmother sitting by his side, warming herself by the fire.

"How are you, Grandmother?"

"I'm fine, my son. It's so good to see you again. How are you?"

"I'm not sure. I'm lonely and I hear Star's voice. Am I going crazy?"

"No, my son, you're not crazy. Her spirit is still with you, and it will be as long as you need her."

"Why did she have to die?"

"I was only strong enough to save one of you, and you were my first concern. I am so sorry about Star. She was a wonderful lady and a great companion, but I promise you my son, you will find happiness again in your life. Trust me."

"I don't know if I can love like that again. She was part of me...part of my blood."

"Trust me, my son. Have I ever lied to you?"

"No, Grandmother, you never have."

The next morning Luke and Storm rode out of the village with Bear at their side. The snow storm was over, but the weather was icy cold and frost was everywhere. Two sets of tracks, one equine and one canine, covered the trail all the way back to Taos. In spite of all that had happened, he was looking forward to sleeping in his own bed.

Luke woke to Bear snoring on the other half of the bed and the smell of Rosita's coffee. He dressed in his buckskin trousers and a heavy wool shirt and his calf-high moccasins. He buckled on his gunbelt and started downstairs. Bear lifted his head and watched him go.

Luke stood on the front porch and sipped on a hot tin cup of joe, and watched the very beautiful Carol Ann Whitley ride up the hill toward the ranch house. He had a strange feeling as he heard his grandmother's words, "I promise you, my son, you will find happiness again in your life."

Luke and Carol Ann talked over coffee and Rosita's sopaipillas. She invited him to dinner and he accepted. They visited for a while before she headed back down the hill. He dressed warmly and headed for town to see Miss Patty to remind her of his promise.

   Follow US Marshal Luke Kash, Bear and Storm in the new Luke Kash Western, *Blood and Thunder*, coming soon.

OLD WEST GLOSSARY

Above Snakes-- still alive.

Barking Irons-- Pistols.

Cayuse-- A cowboy's steed.

Desert Canary-- A burro

Eatin Irons-- Silverware

Fat In The Fire-- To have one's plans frustrated.

Gully Washer-- A hard rain.

Hair In The Butter-- A delicate situation.

Indian Side-- The right side of a horse.

Jimmying A Bull-- Shooting a law officer.

Kansas Sheep Dip-- Whiskey

Leafless Tree-- Gallows.

Made His Jack-- Got what he aimed at.

Nipper-- A baby or small child.

Oats-- To feel one's oats, is to feel one's importance.

Pecos Strawberries-- Beans.

Quincy-- An indoor toilet.

Rig-- Saddle.

Saddle Tramp-- A cowboy who spends his time in the chuck line.

Tarantula Juice-- Cheap whiskey.

Upper Story-- The brain. "He's not right in his upper story."

Velvet Couch-- A cowboy's bedroll.

Walk The Chalk-- Walk straight.

Yer-- You, your, or You're

Books by Duke Charles

Luke Kash Western Series

People of the Horse

Spirit and the Blood

Blood and Thunder

Thunder Cloud and Spirit Walker

Roc Reese Series

Birdies and San Diego Heat

Birdies and Vegas Heat

Birdies and Texas Heat

Other Books by Duke Charles

Duke Charles' Shorts Volume 1

When I Grow Up, I Wanna Be A Cowboy
(Written with Brad Engel)

All books are available, or soon to be available at
DukeCharles.com

Proof

Made in the USA
Charleston, SC
20 August 2016